MY SIDE

BY

KING KONG

AS TOLD TO WALTER WAGER

Simon & Schuster Paperbacks

New York   London   Toronto   Sydney

To Winifred, at last

SIMON & SCHUSTER PAPERBACKS
Rockefeller Center
1230 Avenue of the Americas
New York, NY 10020

First Simon & Schuster paperback edition 2006

SIMON & SCHUSTER PAPERBACKS and colophon are registered
trademarks of Simon & Schuster, Inc.

For information about special discounts for bulk purchases,
please contact Simon & Schuster Special Sales:
1-800-456-6798 or business@simonandschuster.com.

Manufactured in the United States of America

10 9 8 7 6 5 4 3 2 1

The Library of Congress has cataloged the previous edition as follows:
Wager, Walter H.
    My side by King Kong.
        I. King Kong. [Motion picture] II. Title.
PZ4.W128My   [PS3573.A35]   813'.5'4   76-49829

ISBN-13: 978-0-7432-9253-5
ISBN-10:   0-7432-9253-7

INTRODUCTION: THE KONG AND I

I can still clearly remember the first time I met Stanley Harold Kong. (That's his real name. David Selznick himself decided one afternoon to change it to King Kong because it would do better at the box office, but the Old Crowd still called him Stan.) It was 1932, the year before RKO released that terrible picture which made Selznick's name as a producer and ruined my friend's life.

I was the cabin boy on a bucket of bolts called the U.S.S. *Venture,* an aged freighter formerly used to haul guano from Guayaquil to Spokane.

With her hull plates half-eaten through by the acrid guano fumes, the *Venture* was in New York harbor to be sold for scrap when that nut of a producer bought her for $700 in cash plus five percent of the gross profits of any gangster pictures he made. To screw them, he made an animal flick—the greatest in cinema history—and it starred my friend Stan.

It was on the way back from that Pacific island that I got to know Kong. I was assigned by Captain Englehorn to bring chow to Stan down below. Raised to be quite fastidious, always to wash his paws before each meal and after each visit to the toilet, poor Stan had to endure his paws in chains and his ass hanging out the side. (They'd knocked out a few plates, leaving a hole in the hull for Stan to use.) It was hot and smelly below decks, and Stan was miserable. I was desperate to help him, so I opened another hole in the hull to provide some relief with cross ventilation. The Big Fellow really appreciated what I did, which was, to be honest, exactly what I'd do for any 132-foot gorilla with innocent brown eyes. You'd do the same.

I spent several hours a day with him, chatting about all sorts of things, and by the time we reached New York, we were friends.

To this day, he's still loyal to all his old friends, devoted to his family, and deeply grateful to his freaky fans everywhere. Trashy, second-hand accounts of his life have appeared in the *Los Angeles Times*, the *Manchester Guardian*, *Screw*, and the Congressional Record—but none have caught his majesty, his courage, or his fabulous bad breath.

Only he knows the full story—one that will bring a lump to your throat and, perhaps, severe cramps. When you read it you will know why the world thinks of him as a giant and you will applaud . . . or else.

Walter Wager

Hasbeen College
Beckenham, Kent

MY SIDE
BY KING KONG

KING KONG'S OWN STORY

A funny thing happened to me on the way to the Empire State Building, as you may have heard. Here is the whole story: what happened before the movie, the truth about the picture crowd, how I was ripped off, and what I did after that fall off the building—which was, by the way, filthy.

Here are the facts that Big Business and the CIA tried to suppress, plus an unvarnished account of my triumph over alcoholism, bad hearing, atheism, and a hernia that the greatest doctors in television pronounced hopeless.

I was also overweight and a lousy dancer.

Both Merle Oberon and the Statue of Liberty refused dates with me, and crooked judges wouldn't let me see my own children.

The London *Times* barred me from its crossword puzzle, shyster lawyers stole my money, and vicious gossips destroyed my film career by spreading false rumors that I was temperamental, unreliable, and infected with ticks.

Three marriages and four businesses failed, and I went to jail . . . eight times. I was threatened with deportation, vivisection, root-canal work, and nomination as the Socialist candidate for lieutenant-governor of South Dakota.

In addition, my purse was stolen in the Radio City Music Hall . . . during the Christmas show. Several TV commercials and a teaching post at the University of California that should have been mine were lost because of plain and simple racism, and the prime minister of Sweden got up on the floor of the United Nations and held me responsible, personally, for the Vietnam War.

The FBI bugged my bananas, Gore Vidal mocked my grammar, and I was forced to resign my seat in the U.S. Senate when a spiteful secretary spread word that I was a terrible roll in the hay. I pointed out how my hay fever made this whole thing a patent lie, but they wouldn't listen.

Now I'm asking you to listen.

Hear My Side.

I was born on February 29, 1912, a leap year—which may account for my ability to vault across ninety-foot ravines and over highway toll booths. I'm proud of my heritage, despite years of persecution and discrimination. The great melting pot is what made the U.S. of A. so terrific.

Gorilla Power!

There, I said it.

Fur can be beautiful!

Don't laugh. Apes have been exploited for so many centuries that it isn't funny. (And if you snicker, I'll break your roof.) I used to feel that simians weren't as good as other mammals, but that's all changed in the great liberation of the past fifteen years.

Gorillas—come out of your zoos!

Stand up and be counted.

If the gays can come out, if the women can organize, if the blacks can demonstrate, and the doctors can rip off Medicaid, why not Gorilla Lib? Last year's March on Washington, in which we ate all the cherry trees around the Jefferson Memorial and most of the grass near the

Lincoln Memorial, surely showed what we can do if we pull together. Chimps, orangutans, rhesus monkeys, sociology instructors unite! Join your brothers and sisters for a better America!

Why should we furries be pushed around by baldies like Telly Savalas and Yul Brynner? Why isn't there a single gorilla on the staff of *Reader's Digest, Time,* or *Playboy?* The fact that we once had an alligator in the White House merely reflects tokenism, and besides, he was forced out before he could keep any of his campaign promises to the simians. We have taken more crap than the fertile wheat fields of Nebraska. Enough already!

Okay, I was born on February 29, 1912.

I was the product of a mixed marriage, and that was the start of my problems. My mother was a waitress named Saperstein . . . from Philadelphia. The family was poor but honest, hard-working immigrant stock. My grandparents came to this country (steerage, of course) from a place in eastern Austria that is now western Russia, and my mother's father supported his wife and six children by working as a button-hole pickler. (In Europe, he'd been a concert garbage collector, removing trash from the finest theaters and opera houses.) The pickling brine ruined his hands and left him with a debilitating case of acne that eventually killed him. The family was not discouraged, and I hear some of the children didn't like him anyway, especially Milton. My Uncle Milton went to law school on a pin-ball scholarship and now sits on the Supreme Court of Bolivia.

(Only seven years ago I tried to carry out my mother's death-bed wish. "Stan," she moaned, "make something of yourself. Be like your Uncle Milt." I went to the state capital and tried to sit on the Supreme Court. A large part of the cheaply constructed building caved in, killing fourteen people and causing my indictment for manslaughter and malicious mischief.)

My mother's name was Rose. I have seen pictures of her as a laughing, freckle-faced teen-ager; she was lovely. She had big brown eyes and a fantastic ass. She loved Mendelsohn, Debussy, and a man named Blitzer—who happened to be married. (He broke her heart. Mrs. Blitzer broke her glasses.) Mom was also fond of dried fruit, sex, and animals. That's how she met my father. He was working four shows a day in an animal act for the Ringling Brothers. He was a star. Everyone said he had a natural talent for it.

They were right.

He was a gorilla.

He was actually a *Gorilla gorilla*, which is scientific lingo for the lowland branch of the family that's still balling anything that moves in equatorial West Africa. (If you're a geography freak, Our Crowd still swings in southern Nigeria, Cameroon, Gabon, and Guinea.) My father's mother, Harriet, was actually his third cousin by marriage. She wasn't a *Gorilla gorilla*, but a *Gorilla beringei*—an upland or mountain gorilla. They run big, and that could explain a lot about me.

My father's name was Arthur Kong, and he was a good-looking, outgoing, and delightfully charming guy who loved show business and had no head for money. He worked for peanuts, plus an occasional jelly apple, tangerine, or cheeseburger (rare). He had also shown interest in fish and chips and Benjamin Disraeli when the circus was in England. It was my mom who introduced

4

him to dried fruit, and he introduced her to a new kind of love that's still illegal in forty-six states, the District of Columbia, and Spain. It's okay in progressive countries such as West Germany, Denmark, and Japan (except on religious holidays).

Yes, theirs was a forbidden love . . . in Philadelphia.

It was doomed, but beautiful.

Remember the Montagues and the Capulets? That was nothing compared to the hatred between my grandparents. The Sapersteins wanted her to marry a pharmacist, or at least a fish smoker: a professional man. The Kongs wanted their boy to stick to his own kind: something covered with fur and imbued with the traditions of the circus. Even the boss, impressario John Ringling South, predicted that this romance couldn't last.

"I'll kill myself if you don't give her up," Grandma Kong told my dad.

"What do you think, Pop?" dad asked my grandfather.

"Who was listening?"

Dad took grandpa's sound advice, which was hardly surprising since his father had made a small fortune on the ponies and in wheat futures. (It was actually one of the smallest fortunes around: $11.90—which was a lot more in those days.)

Despite all those cheap innuendos in the Rex Reed column and those sly looks on the David Frost interview, the Kongs were not a family of nobodies. They were Big Stuff back in Africa, owning thousands of acres of green forest and a chain of motels and toilets. Grandma's family had a horseradish mine and three thriving cemeteries— one Russian Orthodox. Bodies came from as far as Odessa and Bel Air. My dad was supposed to become an optometrist, but he had the show biz bug—plus amoebic dysentery and ringworm—and he jumped at John Ringling South's offer to join the Greatest Show on Earth.

Grandma was an airline stewardess; she looked great in the uniform but had some problem with the fact that there were no airlines yet. She was always years ahead of her time, terribly creative, and vivacious. "Someday there will be major companies with names like Pan American, British Airways, and TWA," she told her father.

He sent her to a psychiatrist, who recommended that she cut down on her intake of marinated coconuts and take an ocean cruise. It was on the boat that she met grandpa, who swept her off her feet and also stole her navel. When they got to America, he sold it to buy her a polyurethane wedding ring.

It was one helluva love story and the beginning of the plastics industry. There's a factory town in Japan named after my grandmother, and every year on the anniversary of her wedding grateful residents give raw fish and discontinued models of TV sets to any ape in town.

Try to get the picture.

Things were different in the U.S. of A. back before World War I. There was no pasteurized milk, no MacDonalds, not even group sex. No one had ever heard of Frank Sinatra, Agatha Christie, or feminine hygiene sprays. The idea of mixed doubles hadn't reached tennis let alone matrimony and most of the action was still on grass courts or the pool tables of college fraternities.

For a woman to get involved with an ape was unheard of—especially in Philadelphia.

In East Hampton or Malibu maybe, but not in a solid-middle-class part of Philadelphia. Of course, today we

6

can see that Philadelphia, the City of Brotherly Love, was always full of Main-Line WASP hypocrites. What else can you say about a community that okays loving your brother—plain incest, in my book—but locks out decent apes and other animals. It's easy to understand how this repression drove Ben Franklin to Paris, where you can fool around with anyone you please.

All of Philadelphia and most of the circus crowd told my parents that they'd never make it. They did make it . . . several times. I'm the living proof. Love conquers all, and a couple of quarts of cheap red wine doesn't hurt either. There were all sorts of barriers, including body-guards John Ringling South had assigned to keep group-ies away from my dad, the Star. My mother used to sneak in, hidden in a hollow bale of fodder, and this led to the first great roll in the hay in American history. It was an onion roll, my dad's favorite.

"Let's get married," my father suggested one night under a full moon.

"I don't know whether society will let us, Dear."

"Well then, could you tell me where you buy these terrific onion rolls?"

She told him, of course, and never regretted it. Even after the circus left town in the middle of the night (with my fun-loving dad completely smashed on California burgundy), she found a certain quiet comfort in the fact that he'd be able to buy those onion rolls whenever he returned to Philadelphia.

She also found that she was pregnant.

People used to do that.

There were no pills, nasal sprays, or science-fiction movies in those days. Since there were no talk shows in

Philadelphia that paid more than scale, my mom had to turn elsewhere and decided that the only fair thing to her family was to tell her mother. Grandma Saperstein had a fine sense of humor, and when she was in a good mood she often paid above scale. (She tended to chisel on the overtime, but then who didn't?)

It wasn't an easy decision. Grandma had opposed the romance from the start, and she had a tendency to swear a lot in Russian and Austrian. This made my mother nervous, for while she always did well in English and Social Studies she had no head for languages. Playing it safe, she called grandma on the phone.

"Mom, I'm in a delicate condition," she confessed.

"I don't know where that is," Grandma Saperstein replied, "but get the hell back to town. It's Friday night, and I've cooked up a dinner that could kill a Cossack."

(That estimate proved all too correct. Several members of the family suffered gastric strokes, and Uncle Milton later sued in the Small Claims Court.)

Uncle Milton also told my mother that Philadelphia wasn't ready for either color television or a woman-ape baby, and thoughtfully suggested that she haul her ass out of town and never come back.

"But I have no money," she pointed out shyly.

"I'll hock the ambulance," he replied generously. (In training for his future legal career, Uncle Milton had bought an aged ambulance, one used by Teddy Roosevelt in the Spanish American War, which he practiced chasing to develop his legs and wind.)

He took out a second mortgage on this precious vehicle, and it was that money which paid for my mother's ticket on the Orient Express. In 1911 those crazy French ran the Paris-Istanbul trains via Los Angeles and that's

8

where Rose Saperstein arrived on New Year's Day.

The streets were filled with drunken revelers, gamboling among the orange groves and bingo parlors with merry shouts of "D.W. Griffith" and "Up the Hadassah" and "Pass the Sangria."

My mother had a sister living in a suburb, Shirley. (Most of the people who lived in Shirley were relatives of the world-famous Marx Brothers, which is why they were often called Chicanos. Sometimes they were referred to as Marxists, and a number were deported and now serve in the Castro cabinet.) My aunt's name was John Murray Anderson Saperstein, and she was an uncertified public accountant who specialized in tax returns. She was a real pro, doing so well that 98 percent of her returns were returned with fraud charges by the federal authorities.

She welcomed my mother warmly.

"Get lost, Rose," she said with that sweet smile she always had when her upper plate didn't hurt.

"And take your bastard with you."

She threw my mother a Catalina ferry schedule, and my mother threw her a kiss and the remnants of a bacon, lettuce, and tomato milkshake. It was at this point that fate intervened.

When my mother got to the dock, the boat for Catalina was burning and a group of mariachi players was offering a haunting medley of "Did Your Mother Come From Ireland?" and "The Moonlight Sonata." Caught up in the spirit of the moment and a slight touch of morning sickness, Mom staggered over to the next pier and signed onto a freighter carrying Monopoly sets and Kaopectate to Tahiti—where both were in great demand.

"Can you stitch sails, stew prunes, or stoke the boilers

when we tack to starboard?" Captain Ahab challenged.

"No, but I know some great limericks, and I'm used to greasy food," she replied with a toss of her curls and some fancy footwork.

"Why didn't you say you Charleston?" he chuckled genially.

"I tango too."

She was hired as a combination dancing instructor and macrame coach, and also ran the group therapy sessions. Most of the crew respected her deeply, but there were a few who lusted; to avoid them she found it best to sleep in the boiler. She lost sixteen pounds and most of her hair on this incredible voyage, and her skin was pretty well singed too.

Still, she never stopped smiling.

No matter what happened, she kept her upper lip stiff and some snatch of Verdi on her lower lip. This made it tough to eat, so she mostly drank her meals through a straw. Capt. Christopher C. Ahab drank most of his meals too, contributing to a minor course deviation that brought his ship about 900 miles north of its intended destination. To be fair, there was also rotten weather.

Typhoon Desirée.

Hurricane Endora.

Add to this a tidal wave named Fredericka, a rainstorm named Gloria, and a navigator called Henrietta who wouldn't use a compass because it was against his religion, and you can imagine why the tramp freighter missed Tahiti by a wide margin.

Did I mention that this craft was a tramp freighter? It was. Most of the crew were tramps, bed wetters, trisexuals, and ice-hockey players not good enough to play in their native Canada. The first mate, who doubled on alto as the second mate and chaplain, was a heavy smoker, a bully, and an utter degenerate. Rumor hath it that he eventually became a vicar in a small town near Blackpool.

The ship sailed on and on and on.

The Monopoly sets began to rot in the awful heat of the hold, spawning maggots who tunneled savagely through the hotels on Atlantic Avenue. The crew grew surly and broke into the Kaopectate. Discipline was unraveling as fast as the first mate's unisex wig, and Captain Ahab was loading his blunderbuss and counting his change when they sighted land.

It was rather easy to sight.

They'd run aground on the island where I was soon to be born. It was 11:10 AM on the bright clear morning of November 29, 1911; not a cloud in the sky. Visibility was at least six miles, but it should be noted that the skipper was nearsighted, the navigator farsighted, and the second mate spiteful.

My mother couldn't be blamed either. Her view was obstructed by macrame, and the morning sickness was magnified by the athlete's foot that had been troubling her for the past nine weeks.

"Land ho!" shouted Captain Ahab noisily as he hurled a harpoon into one of the hockey players.

"Shut up," advised Mom.

"Land ho!" he repeated.

That was when she hit him was a gallon jug of Kaopectate, ending a friendship but starting a new chapter in her remarkable life story.

My mother was six months pregnant, which gave her a certain resemblance to Carnegie Hall. To put it more discreetly, she was large with child, crazy with the heat, and fed up with the way the crew cheated on the macrame quizzes. Typical of this rum lot was a goalie from the Montreal High School for Auto Mechanics who tried to pass off an eleven-foot hammock as his own work when it was plainly marked "Made by Dwarfs in West Germany."

Grimly aware of her condition and recognizing the dangerous situation, she grabbed the blunderbuss as soon as the captain crumpled to the deck and charged out to confront the other low-lives on the poop. It was then that she heard the strange native music and got her first glimpse of the island.

She was terrified . . . for a moment.

The sound of those drums, trombones, and violas was enough to strike fear into anyone. Then she recognized the lyrics, and she knew that she was safe.

"I love you, Porgy!" poured from the throats of hundreds of badly dressed natives on the beach.

The tenors were exceptionally good, and their smiling faces showed that they were kindly folk who'd respond well to friendship and a little Calamine lotion for their poison ivy. She had no way of guessing that poison ivy was the national sport here, with arson and changing the lights on the coast to cause shipwrecks running second and fourth—there was no third, a strange local custom.

Later, when she understood the medical situation better, she gave them all Kaopectate to rub into their skins as a cure. Within a few days, everyone on the island had constipated pores, and in adoring gratitude, they made her the White Goddess. But we'll get back to that.

If you believe those crap-artists who wrote the script for the picture, the place was called Skull Island. That is an absolute falsehood, reflecting how low a once classy novelist such as Edgar Wallace had sunk by the time he got to Hollywood and Vine. Yes, Wallace and a slick operator named Merian C. Cooper collaborated on this obscene and dishonest travesty which distorted history and helped the Mongols conquer half the civilized world. It's all in the official records of the Nuremberg Tribunal and the Academy of Motion Picture Arts and Sciences.

This same gigantic lie, the identical propaganda technique later used by Hitler and the Committee to Reelect the President, was not only reiterated but also repeated by a supposedly "non-aligned" toy company named Aurora in 1969. Their model kit of me isn't bad, and you ought to buy one since I get eight cents apiece. The words on the box are awful. The Yale kid in the mailroom who pounded them out never interviewed me, and I doubt whether he ever saw the movie. Not sober, anyway.

Get this:

"Seven million years ago a gigantic ape was born on a small island off the Malay Peninsula. While still a baby, Kong's parents were killed by a tyrannosaurus. . . . Kong grew unbelievably large and strong. Savage natives invaded the island, but Kong remained absolute ruler. . . . A movie producer, known for his exciting and dangerous films, acquired a crudely drawn map of Kong's island, Skull Island."

All lies, and it gets even worse if you have the stomach

13

to read the rest of it. Let the truth come out. The people have a right to know. After all these years, why can't the Free World, the Third World, the Fourth Estate, and nuns everywhere be told whether Rosemary Woods is a vegetarian, what happened to the tapes, and how tall Robert Redford really is.

While we're at it, let's stop using abusive and bigoted terms such as Tooth Fairy. What consenting adults do with teeth is their own business—J. Edgar Hoover to the contrary.

And the same applies to hair and toe-nail cuttings.

Okay, let's get to it.

I am *not* seven million years old.

Even Gloria Swanson and Mrs. Churchill aren't seven million years old. Those guys who eat yogurt in the hills of Georgia (Russia) and the wrinkled ladies in Peru who suck on herbs and wash their feet in pisco sours aren't that ancient, and nobody else is either—not even Mount Rushmore or the Loch Ness Monster.

I'm not even one million years old.

I was born in 1912, so you can figure that one out without a pocket calculator. As for being *gigantic* at birth, what the hell is so huge about ten pounds three ounces? Small it wasn't, but you couldn't honestly call it *gigantic*. Buddy Hackett, Orson Welles, and the London Palladium all weighed more when they first saw the light of day, so why all the oohs and aahs? Did I mention Henry the Eighth of England or King Farouk of Egypt or Al Dubin (who, by the way, wrote the lyrics for such big Harry Warren compositions as "Boulevard of Broken Dreams," "Lullaby of Broadway," and "I Only Have Eyes for You")? They all outweighed me at birth, but nobody

14

makes jokes about *them*. Money can hush up anything if you know the right people.

Not seven million years old.

Not gigantic at birth.

Small island? Right, for a change. Not as small as Barbados or the Isle of Wight, but fairly snug. Off the Malay Peninsula? About 510 miles off, if anybody's counting.

But I'm not picky. No fur off my paws. Who minds a little literary license? It's the split infinitives and lousy spelling that send me up the wall. Nobody's teaching our kids the basics these days—not even in the expensive private schools. Half of them have dropped tree throwing, I hear.

My parents were not killed by a tyrannosaurus.

They never owned one.

They were too poor.

According to Mom, dad once had a small collie and a Ford convertible as pets, but no tyrannosaurus. My father never got to the island, of course, although the circus did play a split week in Sacramento each year and sometimes did charity performances for handicapped children on the beach at Cannes.

For the record, my father is still alive and doing his marvelous impression of the Eiffel Tower as the next-to-closing act at the Folies Bergère. He doesn't bathe as often as he might, but he's still vigorous and charming, and very popular with the wives of Japanese tourists who aren't getting much. He and his current wife, the St. Germain des Pres métro station, send me Christmas cards every year.

Frankly, I don't think that this grand old trouper would recognize a tyrannosaurus if he bumped into one on the Champs Elysées—and not because his eyesight isn't what it used to be. A tyrannosaurus would have to be a couple of million years old, and pop always dug young chicks. (Also young cows, polar bears, and cheerleaders from the University of Alabama.)

My mother had a valuable pedigree German shepherd, but when Hitler came to power she traded him for a mink stole. At other times, she had chicken pox, malaria, and some albums of Caruso singing Joseph Stalin's greatest hits—the records ate too much, so she sent them to her sister, Bessie, in Miami Beach.

Mom, bless her fetid soul, never cared much for pets. Yet there were a couple of armadillos she kept around to fight the roaches. As I'll explain later, roaches were a continuous problem on the island. Mom blamed them on those folks on welfare and the giant flying pterodactyls.

"Schmutzig, schmutzig," she'd say as she broomed out the swamp. "We'll never get this place clean until those dirty birds go back where they came from. They're ruining the neighborhood."

These views are not shared by the entire Saperstein family, and have caused substantial embarrassment to her nephew Barry who's a senior speech writer for Jane Fonda and a member of the board of the Scarsdale branch of Friends of the Birds.

Mom's attitudes may have changed too. At least I don't hear her saying such things anymore. Of course, that could be because I don't hear anything too well after that noisy machine-gunning on the Empire State Building, and the fall on my head didn't help much either. I should also mention, in all fairness, that I haven't seen her since she died. However, I never forget her birthday. I get di-

16

arrhea and blinding headaches every April 1—religiously.

My mother wasn't killed on that island.

To keep history straight, it's name was Zumdum Island. The first thing that Mom said when she got a good look at the place was . . . well . . . unprintable. The second thing was a terrible scream, and the fourth (remember, no thirds) was "This is some dump." The faithful natives changed this just a bit to Zumdum, and it has remained that ever since.

Zumdum Island.

The garden spot of the Indian Ocean it wasn't.

To give you some idea of conditions, natives went up to the slums of Calcutta for vacations. The sewers there were luxury resorts for the Zumdum-bells, as they were called by transient explorers.

Expeditions came from many countries, but still the island isn't on any map or nautical chart. That creep who played the hot-shot producer in the flick, Robert Armstrong, made a big noise about this. Winston Balderdash, who led the British expedition sent out by the Royal Gynecological Society, was later knighted by Bette Davis for *not* putting Zumdum on the map; powerful London banks had investments in the area, and they felt Zumdum would cheapen the whole region. The French Academy hushed up the findings of their captain, Jean Gabin, whom they buried in the living hell of an endless series of "B" gangster movies. The Germans kept the island off their regular charts, but included it on the secret charts issued to U-boat skippers. (In 1916, the U-69 commanded by Conrad Veidt [with Curt Jurgens as torpedo officer and Eric Leinsdorf on the mighty Hammond] tried to put a couple of tin fish into the island, but the watertight doors were secure and our pumps held steady as you go.)

We had some Americans too. A woman named Amelia Earhart opened a sort-of-cutesy gift shop near the dinosaur dump, selling aluminum wrap, luggage, and used bandages removed from plague victims on other islands. So far as I know, she's still there and maintains a regular correspondence with Katharine Hepburn and Madame Pasteur. The other Yank was an odd, nervous fellow who wore a brown paper bag over his head and tennis sneakers.

His name was George Crater.

Maybe *Judge* Crater? Hard to recall. He often consulted a book titled *Criminal Code of the State of New York—Illustrated*, but perhaps because of the racy photos. It was this shifty Crater fellow who gave me my first clue as to what was so special about Zumdum Island.

"It has a funny smell," he confided, "and the laundry service stinks."

Maybe so, but we had no street crime, corruption in high places, or threats of governmental bankruptcy.

Going back to the Aurora account, it is also a big fat fib that "savage natives invaded the island." The people who lived there hadn't invaded, and they weren't at all savage. They were a road company of *Porgy and Bess* shipwrecked en route from Chicago to Dallas. As for the "savage" stuff, all that noise was simply a series of endless rehearsals so they'd be ready to go "on" whenever the Schubert office sent help.

And that stuff about me being an "absolute ruler" was garbage too. Let's take it from the top. The freighter was beached, and the *Porgy* company was sore as hell when they found out that it hadn't come to rescue them. They barbecued most of the crew, ate the Monopoly sets for

18

dessert, and smeared the Kaopectate all over their poison ivy as Mom recommended. On her advice, they then began to dismantle the entire ship to make necklaces and other souvenirs that could be sold to visiting submarine officers.

Some of the books and articles, including the big spread Mailer did for *Esquire* and the eight-part series Aldous Huxley wrote for *The New Yorker*, have stated that my mother was a psychiatric social worker when I was born. I don't believe in exaggerating; I'm proud of Mom and what she accomplished despite terrible odds and skin problems.

They finished dismantling the ship, and there was nothing else to do so everyone was out of work. That's how Mom came to be the first welfare investigator on Zumdum, and that's what she was doing, undaunted by the fact there was no welfare system on the island, until three hours before I was born.

Three forty-five PM on a Thursday, right in the middle of one of the finest matinee performances of *Porgy and Bess* ever done west of Hawaii.

I was destined for show business, and I never looked back.

Even though the Kaiser was girding up his loins and stockpiling jockstraps for the imminent holocaust that would be known as World War I, 1912 wasn't too bad a year to be born. Strikebreakers in Chicago were swaying to a lilting new song called "Melancholy Baby," Oxford freshmen were groping Cambridge sophomores to the tune of "The Sweetheart of Sigma Chi," and from Mobile to Natchez and Memphis to St. Joe mobs of emotionally disturbed Daughters of the Confederacy were "Waiting for the Robert E. Lee."

Unfortunately, none of those songs was being sung on Zumdum.

When I was born, a mixed chorus of *Porgy* understudies was lip-synching "When That Midnight Choo Choo Leaves for Alabam" to a scratchy old 78. The regular witch doctor was out on an emergency call, treating a sick rock with acute appendicitis. When acute appendicitis didn't help the rock, he tried a mustard plaster and then three choruses of "Alexander's Ragtime Band." It was touch and go, nip and tuck, fang and claw, and tea and crumpets for quite a while, which was, in my opinion, entirely unnecessary. Any witch doctor who knew his business would have used antibiotic leeches and the verse of "Chinatown, My Chinatown." Today, of course, we have all those great Stevie Wonder songs and for really difficult cases the Leonard Bernstein score for *West Side Story*. There isn't a single sick rock between Manila and

Madagascar, according to the latest UNICEF reports.

Anyway, I was delivered by an understudy who was great on spirituals but weak on obstetrics.

"What seems to be wrong, Mrs. Kong?" he asked nervously.

"Hot water!" Mom screamed.

"How about a little seltzer?"

"Have you got any cream soda?" she fenced shrewdly.

"Not cold."

"I'll settle for a cup of espresso—and go wash your hands, dummy."

"Espresso's extra."

"Bring the check," Mom ordered angrily.

Then she let out a terrific bellow, called for the manager, and gave birth. Quick as a whip, the alert young intern stepped forward and began to slap.

"That's the afterbirth, stupid," Mom cooed.

"How can you tell?"

Mom hit him one of her famous backhand shots, and he agreed to bring the espresso without charge.

Despite his wise-ass remark, I was a beautiful baby.

"He's got a lot of hair," one of the drummers noticed.

"Runs in the family. Where's my espresso?"

The service was never first-class on that island. When the manager brought the espresso, he forgot the lemon peel. That was an omen of all the abuse and prejudice I would endure in later years. While Mom was blistering the witch doctor's understudy with racial epithets and insults deriding his cooking, the manager demanded that she "come up with the bread" or she'd be picketed.

"You gets no bread with one meatball," she tossed back indignantly, right over the shortstop's head into center field. She blew the double play, and someone else stole the song title.

The picketing began, but Mom ignored the chanting as she concentrated on choosing a name for me. William Makepeace Thackeray was already taken, Jean-Paul Belmondo sounded too foreign, and The Beatles reminded her unpleasantly of the roach problem. She decided to name me for her favorite aunt, the rich one.

"Stanley!" she sighed loudly.

There have been many famous Stanleys: The outstanding American baseball player, Stanley Musial; the noted British prime minister, Stanley Baldwin; and greatest of all, the celebrated explorer and female impersonator, Stanley Livingstone.

My Aunt Stanley was well known in Philadelphia, where she had a big reputation as a fruit squeezer and bad driver. A creative individualistic dynamo who could never run with the pack because of her fallen arches, she organized all sorts of community groups including the first Nazi Party unit in Pennsylvania.

Mom had always believed in natural ape-birth, so she was wide awake and rather irritated when I first saw the light of day. Sticking to her progressive guns and cursing a lot, she spurned all suggestions of bottle-feeding. She rejected bottles of Kaopectate, Yardley's after shave, and photo developer and insisted on nursing. I nursed until I was eleven years old—no mean feat if you consider that Mom had left the island when I was nine.

My infancy passed swiftly with the usual minor ailments: cholera, dragon bites, and chronic colic. Mom's love helped me overcome these, and I grew rapidly. I weighed 115 pounds at nine months, gnashed my three-inch fangs in a wonderfully sweet smile, and defecated all over the place. Reluctant to stunt my personality by repressing my nature, Mom put off toilet training until I was nine—when the snakes began leaving the neighborhood in self-defense. Quite a few of the *Porgy* troupe had built canoes months earlier to flee, and several got to Tel Aviv where they opened a dude ranch.

Life wasn't all peaches and cream on that island. It was more rotten bananas and skin fungus. I eventually made friends with the skin fungus, and by the time I was five we played together regularly. My other companions were a giant twelve-legged hermaphrodactyl named Conrad (thirty-eight breasts, five sets of male organs, and a smile a yard wide), an Apache kid who was dynamite on the harmonica, and my best buddy Maxine. Maxine was a twenty-five-square-yard area of quicksand. Everyone said that Maxine was promiscuous, and it wasn't until years later that we found she was a Japanese spy. She made many propaganda broadcasts for Tokyo during World War II.

It was Maxine, not Mom, whom the world knows as Tokyo Rose. (I'm happy to be able to say that Maxine saw several TV shows featuring the Good Rev. Billy Graham while she was in the federal pen, and found God. She is now the chief fund raiser for a fundamentalist college in Oklahoma and goes to church every Sunday in a Mercedes with a "Swing With Jesus" bumper sticker and white-wall radials.)

Maxine *was* sexually precocious.

Who didn't make some mistake as a kid?

If there is such a creature or geological formation, let it cast the first stone or the second spell or the next all-black production of *Sound of Music*. Live and let live, or I'll break your spine, as Mom often sang—she was great with those old-fashioned Canadian lullabies.

The dinosaurs and I were a fun-loving group. We'd play catch for hours with the Pooh-bears, and when we caught them I was always given the white meat. That's one reason that blond chick, Ann Darrow, later caught my eye.

Not my fancy.

It had to happen, I guess.

Why should Zumdum be spared?

Cannon thundered, machine guns rattled, and crappy looking airplanes rained death and candy wrappers everywhere.

Shell holes to the left and right.

Snack bars and latrines in the middle.

"Emetic! Emetic!" agonized heroes gasped beside the shattered vending machines.

The food was that bad. It was better to throw up—and off to the left where there were heaps of muck and meyer.

Icy winds slashed through their tattered airline baggage, and the endless rain was soon knee deep. Maybe two inches below the knee—just a bit higher than last season. The Hun raked their positions (83 and 101, mostly) all day, and when they caught a few desperate winks the sneaky Krauts infiltrated with crabgrass and lima bean seeds. The Kaiser's massed legions smashed forward to the edge of the Marne, where the apparently hopeless French finally rallied.

They took the last two sets 7–5 and 8–6, and that was when the Teutonic cookie crumbled. History records that the cornfed finger-snapping Yanks came in to help in 1917, and they certainly made some important contributions. Maj. Milton Gordon of the Fur and Leather Goods Division pledged $3,500 in the name of his mother and paid every cent. Teddy Mensh contributed an even five grand, but that was a gift from the firm.

I did mention that our peaceful little island was, somehow, bypassed by World War I until 1916 when a German submarine attacked. It was Zumdum's annual Laundry Day, a traditional festival when you washed the breech-clout you'd been wearing all year. Merry children exchanged clothes pins as presents, and the more sober-minded and religious adults did a lot of fooling around while the scenery was being changed. Everyone on the island looked forward to Laundry Day, especially the starch freaks.

The Huns were canny, ruthless, vulgar. On the eve of their great offensive designed to catch Marshal Foch napping at Quiche Lorraine, they struck simultaneously all around the world in a brilliantly coordinated offensive. To this day, brewmasters in Düsseldorf and ear, nose, and throat specialists on the staff at Sandhurst (and on the sauce at West Point) talk about how brilliantly coordinated that masterstroke was.

"It hurt your eyes," one walrus-mustachioed brigadier recalled on the BBC recently.

"Did you cry?" the soft-spoken interviewer asked softly.

"Like a nipper with wet knickers," the silly nit replied.

Men were men, and Huns were Huns, and nobody talked about how lousy their home-lives had been. It was a simpler world, especially in backwaters such as the tranquil pesthole known as Zumdum. We were all laughing and stoning a physically handicapped kindergarten teacher that Laundry Day when the periscope of the U-69 rose silently through the garbage-capped waters off the north coast.

"You're sure it's Pearl Harbor?" asked the twelfth mate (whose aunt was playing pattycake with Von Ludendorff of the Imperial General Staff).

"Löwenbräu," snapped the skipper confidently.

He looked marvelous in that black turtleneck.

"Fire two, four, and five. Hold the mayo on six and send out for more pickles," he ordered savagely.

The torpedoes ran straight and true. Captain Veidt smirked as the tin fish raced toward the unsuspecting island. Actually, it was no big deal to sneak up on Zumdum. As tropical paradises go, it was definitely bottom of the barrel in terms of attention span, price-earnings ratio, and position on the Hot 100 charts.

"A-ha!" leered the leering captain with a leer.

The explosions vibrated through the hull.

Hit!

Hit!

Miss. (Today you'd say Ms., I guess.)

Hit!

The second hit was a ground rule double, which might have led to a score for the Hamburg team if I didn't have such a good throwing arm. From deep center, where I was playing in a lava crater with as cute a little geyser as you ever saw, I grabbed a 300-pound boulder and cut off the runner at the plate with a perfect pitch.

Boom. . . . Boom. . . . Boom.

"Mrs. Kong," a disgusted 234-by-82-by-59-foot dinosaur grumbled, "you're going to have to do something."

"Right on," agreed a nest of cobras.

They all thought that my gassy stomach had produced those blasts, and it wasn't until the island began to list to starboard that the truth became apparent.

They never apologized, and I never forgot that. The

trauma, the pain and shame, are still etched on my memory, burned into my kharma, and engraved on my panache to this day.

The U-69 surfaced, and the gun crew raced to their positions to shell defenseless little Zumdum.

"Coup de grace! Coup de grace!" whined the bloodthirsty fourteenth mate (whose mother-in-law was doing pushups with Von Hasselblad—just across the hall from Ludendorff's place but with cross ventilation).

"You may fire when you are ready, Gridley," the skipper said, ignoring the fact that the turtleneck was starting to itch.

"The name is Forspeis," the gun-crew chief pointed out politely and signaled his dolts to shoot.

By this time, we were on our toes—and our wings. A flight of early-model pterodactyls was knifing through the air toward the Hun craft. Today the U.S. of A. has the F-16s, completely supersonic; back in 1916, we had prehistoric stuff, mostly the A minus 90—entirely high colonic. With white silk scarfs flapping in the breeze, the pterodactyls dive bombed into the face of heavy fire and dumped incendiary bird droppings all over the deck.

In an instant, Veidt's turtleneck was in cinders, and now it was the U-69 that began to list. Panic spread in the officers' ward room, where Hungarian composers had never been popular. Within a minute and a half (Greenwich Mean Time) the U-69 was crash diving, and the attack was over. . . .

Or was it?

To this day, military historians and the road managers of many Japanese rock groups debate whether that failure at Zumdum broke the back and fogged the glasses of the brilliantly coordinated German attack. I can only tell you that our brave pterodactyls felt a lot better after dumping on that sub—but they always did after a good meal. The *Porgy and Bess* crowd was, to be frank, rather annoyed.

"What birdbrain had the dumb idea to attack those nun-raping Huns before they could buy tickets?" demanded the musical conductor.

"*This* birdbrain. And what's so lousy about birdbrains?" challenged the lead pterodactyl.

"What are nuns?" asked his sister.

"Who knew you were doing a matinee on Thursday?" challenged a third.

When you think about it objectively, there was no reason to assume that those cheap-o Krauts would buy good seats. After all, they attacked Belgium on two-fers and tried to make it to Paris cut-rate by flashing phony student Eurail passes.

Even now, the grateful French warmly recall that when the American Expeditionary Force arrived in 1917, every man-Jack paid for his house seat. All right, General Pershing had a pair of press tickets, but he was reviewing for Poison Gas Weekly.

Riffling backwards through the pages of the calendar

in the noble Warner Brothers tradition, let's pick up our hero in 1917. It wasn't easy. I weighed 390 pounds, and I was terribly ticklish. Virgins are. Today's sophisticates may find it hard to believe, but virginity at five was quite common back then. The church was much stronger in those days—and the psalms were a lot better too. There was a terrific moral code that wasn't cracked by Anglo-American Judeo-Christian Army-Navy cryptographers until after World War II. It's called World War II under the Gregorian calendar given us by Gregory the Thirteenth, but under the previous Babylonian calendar it was known as Montreal.

I learned all that at school.

School on Zumdum wasn't exactly like educational institutions elsewhere, for we had no audio-visual aids, government-funded hot lunches, or special classes for the socially disadvantaged. We did have wonderful school spirit, a determination to go to medical school, and a total lack of toilets. With those pterodactyls busy as heretofore described and the whimsical dinosaur kids cutting up capers and an occasional brass player from the *Porgy* band, it wasn't easy to concentrate.

The first problem was to find the school, which was moved every day to avoid those dive-bombing birds. That was solved when the welfare investigator job faded and Mom swivel-hipped her way into the teaching spot.

"No smoking or drinking," warned the chief of the School Board.

"How about extra-marital stuff?"

"Great idea. I like your thinking, Ms. Kong, so let's step around behind this decaying sea monster and get to know each other better."

Mom got the job . . . and a case of body lice the memory of which still crinkles my huge handsome face with a toothy grin. An only child can be lonely, and I used to skip rope with those lice by the hour. Mom was an excellent teacher, even if her cooking was unfit for human consumption.

"You're an ape, dummy, so eat your toadstool parfait and thank your lucky stars. Great mathematicians and political agitators are starving in China. What those little devils would give for one bucket of that slop."

How was I to know that one of those starvers was to become world famous as Chairman Mao, another to delight children everywhere as Edith Piaf? With trick photography and wonderful makeup, it's impossible to tell that she's the daughter of a Shanghai ping-pong table salesman. Who cares? She's a great public servant and a mar-vel-ous mother.

Which brings us back to Mom.

(Neat, ha?)

Some mothers have a way with children, right? Most of them—aside from a few who punch and kick a lot because they were molested by foster parents, mailmen, and stamp machines.

Okay, here it comes.

Mom didn't have a way with children.

But. (It's a big "but," like hers.) She had a way with prehistorics. With pterodactyls, superb. With all kinds of dinosaurs, fantastic. With giant flying serpents, copy editors, and lava flows only so-so, but nobody's perfect.

She did a "kitchy-coo-you-poor-things-Aunty-Rose-digs-you-the-most-huge-beaks-and-all" act that really flipped the big birds. She stopped the attacks on the

31

school by cleverly bringing the pterodactyls into the process, writing up special material and a piece of choreography to close the first act that featured them. So we all went to kindergarten together, skipping, singing, reading, ripping, rendering, and laughing as we learned that it takes all kinds and everything is beautiful—even sinus infections.

It wasn't a snap. There were troublemakers, including a tyrannosaurus who stole other people's lunches and belched a lot during the intensive finger painting, making it even harder for the rest of us to paint the fingers. It was tough enough for Mom to pry those fingers out of the tight-fisted School Board, and this clown was messing up the whole class.

We had it out one noon in the athletic swamp. He was asking for it.

He? She? Hard to tell with a tyrannosaurus.

"I'm going to take your lunch, Half-Breed," he roared arrogantly.

How that stung! I knew there were other illegitimates who were part-Jewish, creative types such as Edith Piaf. (I'm not sure about Sarah Bernhardt.) Still, the insult smarted. Apes are very sensitive to rejection and scalding water, and brood a lot when the government investigates the Teamster pension funds.

Half-Breed? How many nights have I cried myself to sleep with that taunt haunting my consciousness? It wasn't fair. My father was an agnostic for most of his life, but I've always believed in Easter Sunday, reincarnation, church picnics, and the Archbishop of Canterbury's tips on the Derby.

Why are people—and prehistoric monsters—so cruel?

"Hand over that lunch, Shaggy," he jibed. Or did he tack?

Then he pointed, and I got mad. That wasn't my lunch. That was my mother, in a pale-green two-piece drip-dry pants suit of sheer poison-ivy. Simply stunning.

Now I roared, and for the first time, I beat my chest. I broke two drawers in the process, but it certainly made that snotty tyrannosaurus sit up and take notice. I looked to the right, faked to the left, and kicked him right where he lived. What a vile smell he let out, but I didn't fall for it. Using a bolo punch I learned at a party at Norman Mailer's brownstone in Brooklyn, I knocked the old ty off balance, then, gave him the one-two-four, and dropped him to his knees.

"You crazy or something?" he whinnied.

I could see that I'd battered the fight—and most of his breakfast—out of him, so why stop now? Mom had taught me always to stomp 'em while they're down. I did, and he was a very different tyrannosaurus when he dragged his tail in two days later. "If you can't eat 'em, join 'em," he explained as he hung up his blazer—and he never made any more trouble.

Mom was impressed.

"I saw what you did the other day," she said as we swung home through the jungle after class, "and that was *some* bit with the banging on the chest."

"Thanks, Ma."

"One thing I want to ask you, and tell the truth."

"Sure, Ma."

"You crazy or something?"

I sort of smiled Gary Cooper-style and pawed the dirt. (That hole was later used as a swimming pool by the

173rd Battalion of the Imperial Japanese Army, known as The Sneaky 173rd in 1942. They all wore sneakers, camouflage foulards, and Babe Luth T-shirts.)

We all had a great time at school, and even though we were poor and the neighborhood was definitely shabby, many of my classmates rose above their humble origins. The pterodactyls rose first, as you might expect of ambitious types with fifty-foot wings. Two of them became very prosperous weather balloons in the Philippines, and another is about to retire after a distinguished career as an airborne command post for the Strategic Air Command.

Not all of us made it up the ladder of success.

Take the snakes.

Nobody would. Just because they were poisonous and had crushed a few hundred oxen, small hills, and non-singing extras, employers ran screaming. Locked out of the job market by their childhood pranks, and carrying the stigma of an alcoholic mother, they never had a chance. They tried. Climbing ladders was terribly difficult for them, and nobody thought to offer Montessori training.

Only one of these homicidal but basically decent reptiles broke out of the ghetto. Douglas took a correspondence course in air-conditioning repair, and now heads an encounter group near Washington. Sharp-tongued, trendy, and federally funded, he's been subpoenaed by a number of grand juries and still sends home Christmas bundles of Hilton hotel stationery for the less fortunate.

Remember Conrad, the winsome hermaphrodactyl? He swam out under cover of the U.S. naval bombardment in 1944, gave Admiral Halsey the location of all the Nip's gun positions, and was gratefully commissioned on the spot. As an attack transport, I think. His first marriage to Central Park failed, but now he's settled down in New England and lives quietly as the sports staff of the *Boston Globe*.

Some of the others who ended up walking, swimming, and flying that Last Mile in the Death House could have been productive members of the community. Anyhow, that's my opinion. I try to avoid recriminations, diesel locomotives, and junk mail, but I've got to say that a number of those unfortunates were shafted by Society itself.

To be blunt, quite a few were ruined by those pious missionaries. I have never bad-mouthed the supreme deity, bingo, or church bazaars. I loved T.S. Eliot's *Murder in the Cathedral*, the TV series about the Flying Nun, and the way Southern Methodist ran from the split-T. I still choke up when I hear "He's Got the Whole World in His Hands," even if the top jazz critics prefer "I've Got the World On a String." One of my three best friends is a Buddhist monk, and I've bought every one of those mysteries about the rabbi-detective.

God is A-O.K. in my book. Some of his sales staff, though, really gross me out.

Not all the missionaries were creeps, of course. Just some of them, and they were a disgrace to His/Her entire operation.

They not only messed up a gang of my pals. That's not what I'm sore about, Baby. They wrecked property values, and that's why I left organized religion.

The crooked bingo games didn't help either.

35

Maybe they didn't send out the First Team as missionaries to Zumdum, Mom suggested charitably the night before she bugged out with a Polish anthropological research team.

Poor Mom. Drowning in compassion and the by-products of one diseased kidney, she simply wasn't smart enough or tough enough to cope with the real world—the twentieth-century jungle of pay toilets, male chauvinists, and counterfeit Irish coffee topped by faked whipped cream from a spray-can. She was a loser, one of the many victims of aerosol bombs and polyester election promises. In a word: an idiot.

How could she dream for one moment that those biggies in St. Paul, St. Patrick, and St. Morris would deliberately send *anyone* to Zumdum? The stinking pest-hole wasn't even on the map, so any missionaries who arrived floated in by accident.

You ask how the Supreme Enchilada up there could make such mistakes. With the best-staffed bookkeeping and personnel departments in the universe, how could Numero Uno screw up?

The answer is simple, for those who have faith.

God works in mysterious ways . . . and also takes off a lot of "personal" days.

That's how we always got the bottom quarter of the class, overweight, rheumy-eyed, dirty collars, and very poor public speakers. Mumblers—that's what He/She sent us. Green kids who only knew four or five commandments, old winos who could no longer handle the teleprompter, Salvation Army trumpet players who'd lost their lip, and a few super-righteous types who hated sinners and musical comedies—even Gershwin. They made the *Porgy* group feel terribly guilty.

Some also tried to make the *Porgy* troupe itself. (Themselves, to be grammatical.)

We had few visitors, and the first missionary to arrive was warmly treated. Actually, he was cooked (at 298° celsius) by an overenthusiastic young geyser rushing forward to be baptized. Instead of a conversion we had a buffet, with the usual octopus dip, hayfever and pebble salad, and finger sandwiches provided by the late guest of honor. Whatever his faith, he was delicious.

You can see that our first impression of these men of the cloth was favorable, even if the woman who played Bess complained that the buttons stuck in her teeth. (Things got worse when zippers became popular.)

I'm not wholly sure that the next fellow really *was* a missionary. Do missionaries wear masks, ride out of the sea, and carry six-guns? He showed up on the south shore one afternoon, right in the middle of the macrame championship. Manners were not his strong point. Before I could introduce myself, he began asking questions.

"Okay, who's the jerk who put that saw-toothed reef out there?"

"Charlie Finley," I answered truthfully. "He's terribly innovative."

"Would you take a look at what that damn thing did to my trusty steed's right rear tire?"

That's when I got a funny feeling about this chap. His

glorious white stallion had no right rear tire. He was riding a three-tire horse.

"Would you like a flat seltzer?" Mom offered.

He didn't answer her either.

"Did you see a wonderfully loyal but runty Indian named Tonto?" he demanded.

"How about a clean Javanese girl named Bella who could bring back your manhood?" I suggested.

"Don't take the Lord's name in vain!" he replied and fired off two shots. Then he galloped back impetuously into the garbage, and we did a neat three-part harmony on "Toot, Toot, Tootsie Goo 'Bye" until the surf covered his head.

"Who was that masked man?" Bella wondered as she adjusted her halter. (It was a British Army cavalry halter, which often cut her mouth because it was two sizes too small.)

"Orthodox, I think. The Orthodox wear masks," volunteered my mother.

What the hell did she know?

A gall bladder big as all outdoors, but she never even graduated from high school and had no fur to speak of. Out of respect, we never spoke of it but concentrated on smutty stories. Those were my bedtime stories. It was these same funny yarns that later got her that shot on the Ed Sullivan show and the two-week booking at London's Talk of the Town.

I'm not going to contradict my mother, but I doubt whether that nut was a cleric. But the next cleric we saw was definitely a nut.

Nudity was his obsession. Topless made him wild.

He came in on a balloon on Christmas Eve—an odd

salami-shaped craft with Siberian markings down one side and "Win With Wilson" on the other. I was unsure whether he meant Woodrow, Harold, or Meredith (who did *The Music Man* and the "Iowa Fight Song" and spelled it Willson). Mom had taught us that bad spelling is a sign of impure thoughts, and a missionary with impure thoughts could be a problem.

He started with questions too.

"What's for dinner?"

I didn't trust him from the start. There hadn't been any Serbia for at least five years, and what the hell was he doing wearing a Jimmy Carter button when Carter hadn't been born yet?

But I was willing to give him a chance. After all, he might have money.

"Belly up to the cauldron, Padre," I invited, "and stuff your puffy face with all the slop you can handle."

That was when he started hollering.

I thought it was a cheer at first.

"B . . . O . . . S . . . O . . . M . . . S . . . Sinny! Sinny! Sinny!"

It was all in the Bible, he explained. Old Testament, New Testament, and the Book of Prudes, chapter 11.

I thought that chapter 11 covered bankruptcy and champerty, but he easily convinced most of us that it also meant, if interpreted symbolically, heresy, killing butterflies out of season, and exposing your assets before a blind man on the King's Highway.

You simply cannot imagine the difficulty he had in getting those dinosaurs to wear bras. The entire costume department of the *Porgy* company worked around the clock to get the job done. It was, to be precise, a Mickey

39

Mouse wristwatch, but who cared? God's Will is the big thing, right?

Shame.

The island was crotch deep in shame, prurience, morbidity, cracked nipples, and guilt within weeks. I didn't understand all the weeping, moaning, stitching, basting, and preaching. Lord, how that man did preach! Every day was Sunday, and the endless outpouring of sermons got to be a drag because Zumdum operated on a four-day week. Local custom. Day and night services, with threats, hand-gestures, and frequent passing of the hat.

It was eleven weeks before we discovered that the goodiest-good-good minister had something else going most nights after prayers. Fooling around with the hermaphrodactyl, who had so many of everything. We threw him out, nicely.

"Listen, Phil," Mom told him as she picked him up by the scruff of the belly, "we don't blame you. Only human. There's a lot more action over on the next island—about 205 miles northeast by southwest as pterodactyls fly. Place called Corsica. Wonderful linguine, and a girl named Sadie Thompson who needs saving in the worst way."

"That's my way," he said, and he kissed her permapress ring. (I believe they call it ring-around-the-collar in some countries.)

There were other missionaries, including some fine dedicated types who taught us the Book of Numbers and sold them, one who sang well and coached basketball even better, and another who ran superb services but wouldn't let any of us attend because we weren't worthy.

"Don't let it depress you, Stan," Mom said as she

packed to abandon me. "He's a foreigner. You can tell by the accent."

Her parting advice has served me well. A mother knows.

"Wash more often," she said tenderly, "and stay away from malignancies and earthquakes. They can ruin your life. You can go all the way, Stan—right to the top!"

How could she have guessed about the Empire State Building?

The answer is older, bigger, and funkier than both of us. A mother *always* knows.

She took off, unaware that the idea for the movie was already percolating in the coffeepot of an incredible Hollywood caffeine-freak named Merian Coldwell Cooper. It was Merian Coldwell Cooper—journalist, World War I combat flier, author, screenwriter, and cinema visionary—who had the dream of making a picture about a giant ape.

They all laughed at him as a fool.

They were right.

First of all, let me go on record that Cooper had a lot of guts and a good mind and more class than most of the pizza-burgers running the studios today. He was a real pioneer in filming on location in exotic places, and he was fascinated by all kinds of animals. They had some toughies in Hollywood in the 1920s, guys who'd make today's moguls look like ninety-eight-pound weaklings, the kind who wear white cotton socks all the time.

You know what I look like?[2]

Tall, well built, graceful with a wonderful Jimmy Stewart smile and all my hair.

Well, here's what Cooper looked like, according to the deftly-written autobiography of Marguerite Harrison who went to Iran with Cooper and his partner, cameraman-director Ernest V. Schoedsack, to shoot a picture called *Grass*. He was "short, muscular, and thickset; with sparse sandy hair; a sharp, pointed noise; eyes like blue China buttons; a pugnacious jaw; and an aggressive manner."[4] In case you can't imagine how such a living doll was the genius behind a picture that ruined my career and those of giant gorillas everywhere, the lady said he was also stubborn, moody, quick-tempered but generous.

Sounds like Pat O'Brien, doesn't it? Jimmy Cagney?

Not much resemblance to the moguls such as Harry Cohn, Louis B. Mayer, Darryl F. Zanuck, J. Arthur Rank,

[2]Sic.
[4]Very sic.

42

Samuel Goldwyn, Adolph Zukor, or the other dynamos who broke so many hearts and box office records in movieland. Well, what could you expect from a short man with sparse sandy hair who cared more about movies than taxshelters, points, or starlets stashed in the broom closet of the Polo Lounge—the fashionable riding stable of the fashionable Beverly Hills Hotel. Cooper, who's reputed to have dated Beverly Hills before she went high hat, made pictures, not deals.

Even though he was a bit freaky about dragons and extremely tall gorillas, I kind of liked him, and we kept in touch over the years. Remember the mysterious veiled woman in black at his funeral in 1973? That was me.

It was Cooper's cockeyed idea that a flick about a "terror ape" would grab movie audiences by the shorts, and the stuff coming out of RKO in 1929 and 1930 wasn't doing that at all. Several producers were thinking of returning to the fur business, and one major executive was already selling off swatches of office furniture through his wife's thrift shoppe. Like the rest of the country, RKO-Radio Pictures was on the ropes. If the tiny daughters of Wall Street brokers were jumping off the roofs of their doll houses, the corporate directors at RKO were nearly as twitchy.

It was the Depression, so they were Depressed.

Nobody ever claimed that those bankers and money men were original. They were always afraid of anything new, swift to imitate but scared to originate. Is it any wonder that the Danes were the first with porno and dark beer? Well, Cooper spent more than two years selling the idea to D.O. Selznick who shrugged a lot in his camel's-hair jodphurs, swung his mink riding crop abstractedly, and inadvertently scarred Miss Antarctica of 1930 for life.

"Don't worry about it. It's only a small country," he's said to have told Cooper.

There's another version in the Museum of Modern Art's classic sixty-two-volume study titled *Cinema, Ho: the Great Producers, Proctologists, and Head Cases of American Film.* In her definitive chapter on Selznick, Amanda Shikell tells us that Selznick's blacksmith was in the office shoeing a favorite polo pony and that taciturn Scot recalled the incident quite differently.

"Easy with the sparks, Jock."

"Yes, Mr. David."

Then Miss Antarctica, a mischievous sprite, bounced across the roof to relight the producer's cigar and ran into the riding crop. The fourth and fifth slashes were his efforts to close the wounds.

"Will you sell my ape picture to the Board, D.O.?" Cooper pleaded as he tore his shirt into bandages with one hand and splashed a better-than-fair 1927 Pommard on the gashes with the other.

"Why not?"

"Then I'll adopt her as my daughter, D.O., and I'll pay for the plastic surgery."

"We'll pick up half the tab, kid," said Selznick who was as generous as he was talented. At that point, he brought out his good crystal—the Waterford left over from *The Informer*—and the three of them polished off the Pommard. (Shikell records that the pony drank a rather ordinary 1930 Vouvray, which the many admirers of the great D.O.S. may find difficult to believe.) The girl later had, after she learned to run on all fours at the Actor's Studio, a dazzling career as Lassie.

Selznick went to New York and gave a great pitch for

44

the picture to the members of the RKO Board.

"That was a curve," said Mendelson impassively as he patted his seeing-eye dog.

"Let's not be hasty," urged Kittridge. Kittridge, a banker with a crew cut and a son flunking snow-shoveling at Dartmouth, was the voice of moderation and had a rich wife.

"Why do you think this stinker won't stink?" challenged Birnbaum—who had an even richer wife and a stool on the Stock Exchange. He could have easily afforded a couch, but that seemed ostentatious.

"Rin Tin Tin!" Selznick said softly.

In case some of the Board members had missed this crusher, he pounded his riding crop on the table and repeated the magical name. They all looked up at him, a magnificent figure on his pony. He cantered around the room twice, letting his genius sink in.

Rin Tin Tin was one of the hottest stars in the business, with a body temperature three degrees above Jean Harlow. Of course, that fur coat helped, but nobody could deny that the mutt was a b.o. bonanza.

"If one animal works, try another."

"Boffo!" shouted one avaricious financier.

"Harpo!" yelled another.

"Sacco and Vanzetti!" chimed in a third—the liberal who respected their spunk even if their grammar wasn't much.

"One of your greatest ideas, Dave," complimented Mendelson, "but of course you aren't going to let this jerk Cooper write the script."

"My niece, Antigone, scribbles a bit," Kittridge confided modestly.

"I want to save her for something bigger—maybe

45

Grapes of Wrath or *Hello, Dolly*. No, I'm thinking of Edgar Wallace. He's a world famous novelist, a Protestant, and English."

"Go, Baby, go!" urged Birnbaum as he rose to call his wife.

Wallace was internationally known as the author of many first-rate thrillers, one of the top three or four creators of cops-and-robbers yarns during the first three decades of the century. He was known to work fast; his penmanship with the old quill was elegant . . . and he happened to be under contract to RKO. (He also happened to be in terrible health.) Fast? He did a 110-page treatment in five days. This cat did 170 novels and seventeen plays before pneumonia grabbed him. Cooper found only a few chunks of the treatment that coincided with his own ideas, so he wrote a very different screenplay. The final draft reflected the substantial talents of the wife of the co-director/co-producer. In the greatest traditions of twentieth-century filmmaking, she was shafted and initially got no screen credit whatsoever.

She deserved it.

She was the one who thought up that bit on the Empire State Building, and she's the broad I'll never forgive. It isn't sexism. I'd feel the same way about a man.

But let's get to the picture.

Let's talk about the important stuff first.

Money.

Cynical? No, that's what I've learned from the Hollywood crowd, the barons of Bel Air who run the industry.

It isn't art to those babies—all bottom line. To that crowd, Truffaut is a mushroom you find in imported chopped liver and Fellini is a kinky kind of you know what.

Whatever else you might say about the RKO biggies, they did spend a few bucks on my first picture. Of course, Selznick was running the lot and vaulting the furniture . . . and David O. was never cheap. He went for the best. When he wed, the lady, a fine person with good ankles and great jewelry, was none other than the wise and sensuous daughter of Louis B. Mayer. Mayer was the lord of MGM and it was Lovable Louis—not the lion—who ruled as King of the Beasts. He himself was a genuine tycoon, and he wasn't cheap either.

He was quite a few other things.

Going back to Selznick, he didn't stint on the budget for the ape extravaganza. It took about a year to make the picture, and the production cost was more than $513,242[6] —a tidy sum in 1932. They must have spent a lot of it on promotion, trick photography, special effects, whole sides of Scotch salmon, and jeroboams of Dom Pérignon. I sure

[6]Two cents more, to be precise.

didn't see a nickel,[7] and they certainly didn't spend much on those actors.

Frank Sinatra once told me that it's poor taste to bad-mouth another performer, and I've always respected his taste, judgment, and lawyer (who was one helluva tackle for UCLA[8]). However, I've got to say that Bruce Cabot was no Lord Larry Olivier. Nice kid, good teeth—a real cornball. Worst damn haircut I ever saw. I think his elbows were his best feature, that and his politeness. He never screamed when Selznick got a bit excited with that riding crop.

There are plenty of other good things you could say about Brucie, and I'll remember them in just a second.

Right.

He was neat, and he brought his lunches in a brown paper bag.

He didn't suck his thumb on camera.

He rarely wet his pants or stole pencils from Wanda, the two-headed script girl.

He had no desire to play Hamlet or Jimmy Connors, realizing that either could kill him.

He wasn't afraid of malaria or any of the other tropical diseases that he couldn't spell.

He laughed a lot at funerals, proving that he had a boy-ish sense of humor and a lust for life.

He wasn't envious, anemic, or shrewd enough to argue about money . . . and he never signed petitions supporting Loyalist Spain, Fidel Castro, or fluoridation of water.

---

[7] The brontosaurus got $10 a day, and had to bring his own costume.

[8] Scout's honor.

Brucie was a swell kid and the whole crew was terribly fond of him, but he was no great actor. What's more, the ruthless moguls tended to dump him into flicks that were garbage. They called it "product." (Product is what you make so the projector won't catch a cold by a sudden chill when there's nothing to show.) He was in auto-racing pictures where the carburetors were the stars and he was the boy ingénue. In one of his prison flicks the electric chair got more money than he did *and* better billing.

Brucie was in pictures that were so unbelievable that Ronald Reagan got the girl and Brucie got trench mouth. He could punch and smile enough for simple action parts, but the boy really couldn't play male leads. The love scenes were so embarrassing that the ushers walked out.

Still, he worked in all kinds of pictures and almost never hurt himself.

I've got to be careful about what I say about Fay Wray. She wasn't too bad in Erich Von Stroheim's *The Wedding March*. Only a fair puncher, she could act her way out of a thin paper bag—despite what Hedda and Louella told Rex Reed. They were just jealous of her youth, her big eyes, and her fine legs.

She had one good cheekbone (left), a great right arm, and enough on the cameraman so he always filmed her better side.

The outside, as I recall.

She was one of the most dedicated, decent, and respectable stars of that marvelous era. She never beat her servants, abused Fatty Arbuckle, or went to orgies unless there were two separate sets of dishes. A stickler . . . on her mother's side, a McInerney on her dad's.

She was a great favorite of the crowned heads of Europe, and often ran at Epsom and Ascot and Longchamps.

She loved her children and was such a good mother that adoring fans frequently mobbed her palatial bungalow.

Fay Wray was an aristocrat, certainly no tramp.

A hobo—maybe. She looked good in gamine suits . . . and also Chinese Chippendale. The fact is that she wasn't Cooper's first choice for the part. Jean Harlow was the sex symbol he originally had in mind, and I could have gotten something good going with her. That was a hunk of broad.

It's never been made clear why they switched and offered the role of Ann Darrow to Fay, but I have a theory. Jean Harlow wanted cash, and maybe even a script.

(Did I mention that another writer named James Creelman gave the screenplay a bit of a brush too? It was more of a wax, I'm told, but eventually his name and that of Ruthie Rose graced some prints.)

Fay wasn't just a game kid with good gams and a fabulous scream, although it is absolutely true that she howled so long and so well for this film that pieces of recorded scream were later interpolated in other pictures.[9] RKO didn't waste anything, not even the paper plates. Two members of the crew of the *Venture* were originally paper plates. Both of them acted better than the ham[10] who played Carl Denham—the filmmaker with bad dialogue and worse breath.

After this picture, Little Faysie had a worldwide reputation as a fraidy-cat, and a lock on the best horror pictures.

Still, she could act and tap dance and ignore the rude

[9]I didn't make this up.
[10]Always gave to the Red Cross though.

language of the common seamen. I never got to know the ship's crew that well, but I noticed one thing. Maybe you spotted it too. They wore hats almost all the time.

Think about it.

Tropical island.

Hot and humid.

Jungles and swamps.

Hats?

Hats on deck . . . day and night.

Hats when they came ashore that first time looking for a bathroom.

Hats when they returned after midnight to try to rescue Ann from the fate-worse-than-death.

Why?

Cooper told me in 1968, when we met at the urologist's.

"King," he reminded me with an affectionate punch to the ankle, "it was 1932 and RKO needed outside financing badly. That was back before all the government money was available. Today, you could get a couple of mil out of the CIA by saying you were funding an anti-Commie coup to liberate the island from Red peckerwoods."

"We had pterodactyls, but no peckerwoods," I protested.

"Don't protest. They'll put you on a list as an agitator," Cooper warned warmly. Wormed wornly? . . . He was tired.

"But we didn't have any peckerwoods," I whispered agreeably in a low, thunderous roar.

"The CIA could lend you some. They've got plenty in a secret peckerwood depot at a classified location. Fresh or frozen, take your pick."

"What the hell would I do with a frozen peckerwood?"

"They make wonderful paperweights."

"Hats?" I reminded.

He shook his small, sparsely-haired head.

"No good for hats. They drip. Oh, the money. RKO hadn't been bought by Howard Hughes[12] yet."

"What's he got to do with peckerwoods . . . or hats?"

"He manufactured the basic model—the P-1 all-weather peckerwood—for the CIA. Anyway, RKO needed cash so they turned to the underworld . . . the hat mob. They sold out their ideals for cash."

I looked shocked.

"Don't look shocked, Big Fella. Hollywood does that to a lot of people. A secret cartel of major hat manufacturers agreed to finance the picture if we'd slip in a lot of pro-hat propaganda. It was one huge commercial!"

Suddenly I remembered those reporters and press photographers at the theater the night I was chained up. They all had hats too. I yield to no one in my contempt for the sartorial and literary taste of the American press, but those skimmers were the worst. Even the hoods in the Jimmy Cagney movies wore better toppers.

"So all those sailors wore hats because the fix was in, Merian?"

"A couple were bald, and RKO was too cheap to rent toupees. Don't look at me that way, King. I fought hard to salvage what I could. There was one beret manufacturer from Chicago—with French connections and 348,000 size 6¼'s he couldn't unload—who wanted to meet little Fay. I told him where to go.

"Yes?"

[12]See *My Secret Affair with Howard Hughes* by Herman Goering, page 711.

"She'd moved out to live with her sister. Fay was as pure as the driven snow, no mean feat in southern California in July. I've seen her drive snow 210 yards, with a three iron—wearing only her army shoes and that spunky smile."

I checked it out, aware that memories fade over the years and old men tend to exaggerate. It was a four iron, and artificial snow.

How little we know.

How soon we forget.

Okay, 1932 and we were having our little problems on Zumdum too. Over-production of our basic crop and a glut of cheap Japanese imports had ruined prices, forcing farmers to the wall.

The island's basic crop has always been roaches, and we just couldn't compete with those transistorized Japanese models. The wall that I mentioned was one that we prehistoric monsters had put up to keep out the roaches. Maybe the show biz crowd found them lucrative or cute, but we had our own cozy ghetto and we didn't want our traditional way of life threatened by outsiders moving into the neighborhood. As soon as we put up our wall, the *Porgy* troupe started building barbed-wire fences all over the place to protect the sheep.

We tried to accept their new ways, but it wasn't easy for the old timers to understand.

There were no sheep on the island.

Try to explain that to a 900,000-year-old tyrannosaurus who's set in his ways.

Cooler heads on both sides—and one grizzled sea serpent with three heads and chrome fins just like a '56 Cadillac—tried to make peace. Presents were exchanged as gestures of good will. We gave them rotten dinosaur eggs and Rudy Vallee records, and they sent over assorted hors d'oeuvres—Italian salami, barbecued ribs, green olives, and teen-aged girls. I ordinarily like such simple finger food, but the girls were a bit fatty and the grass skirts tasted like straw.

But I didn't complain.

Trying to be a good neighbor, I ate whatever the show folk served and never complained about the fifteen percent service charge.

That was the situation when the idiot skipper of the *Venture* dropped his anchor and upper plate off our south-northwest coast. Some people say that Captain Englehorn wasn't half bad, but if that's true why didn't he ever dare to remove his hat? I believe he was a Nazi spy, with a swastika tattooed on his scaly scalp. Even Selznick never contended that Captain Englehorn was charming, not nearly as gracious as Captain Spaulding or Field Marshal Rommel who threw fantastic parties with great door prizes.

Englehorn drank.

Why deny it?

The crew was all non-union, including the weirdo navigator and the sound man. They were the dregs of waterfront dives in Tangier, Kowloon, Rio, and Denver . . . and they had a terrible prejudice against prehistoric monsters. In fact, they didn't like historic monsters either. These were the goons who snuck onto our island, armed to their rotting teeth with repeating rifles that should have been sold to Geronimo.

It was a Wednesday, so the orchestra was tuning up for the matinee. Those were the "savage drums," and the wild "ceremony" that Denham tried to film was the usual opening number of *Porgy*.

Gorilla skins? Balderdash. Sure, the costumes were a bit shabby after twenty-one years of continuous performances—the longest running musical in Off-Broadway history: 8,736 performances of which several were sold-out to theater parties. As a matter of fact, before the tensions about the roaches caused certain hot-heads to push for that wall I used to drop by at least once a week.

I hate false modesty as much as I despise welfare frauds, so I might as well admit that I was extremely popular on Zumdum. Monsters and people just sort of cottoned to me in those days, and even now there are millions all over the hectic modern world who still polyester at the sound of my chest-thumping. Back in '32, everyone connected with the performing arts on the island recognized me as a kindred monster, so I never paid for a ticket.

Strictly cuffo.

All freebies, compliments of the management.

Whenever I showed up, they always found a nice block of thirty-five seats for me in the fifth through the tenth rows. I saw *Porgy and Bess* so many times I knew the whole score. There was one night when one of the stars and his understudy were both out with jungle rot, and I was asked to step in and play Sportin' Life with aplomb.

"I'd rather use my own racquet, sir," I bellowed politely.

"Use the plomb and don't argue," replied the director.

I wasn't about to argue with this man, so respected and deranged that even the rabies germs didn't dare tangle with him. I used the plomb, and the critic for the *Times* wrote that my performance was "larger than life, original, and an interesting blend of vigorous and deafening." I don't know whether you read that review, but I definitely saw him cork the bottle and toss it into the eastbound current.

When the usual Sportin' Life and his understudy returned in bandages two days later, they told everyone that it was no fun being out with jungle rot because her husband was insanely jealous and a vicious philatelist. I played the part for seven performances—to standing applause. By the fourth, I had the choreography down cold and they were all cheering for Ole Twinkletoes. At one matinee, half a dozen attractive masochists on the board of the Suicide Club rushed the stage, tossing bouquets of rotting fish in a girlish effort to win my rage. Bowing gratefully, I lobbed the odoriferous offal off into the wings with a jaunty flip of my immense wrist.

I must have put too much spin on the flip, because I later heard that the Japanese Air Force scrambled three squadrons of fighters (with a little cheese and chopped onions) to defend Tokyo.

Generally, performances of *Porgy* were uneventful if not boring and on several occasions they had to paper the house by slipping free tickets to the roaches.

"Why not paper the roaches?" I suggested helpfully.

"Then they'd be in the walls."

This seemed to make sense . . . at first.

Later I noticed there were no walls, except our barrier designed to keep those low-income interlopers out of our fashionable swamp. We'd already done that wall with Toulouse-Lautrec posters, obscene underwear ads from the Sunday *Times* and the London tubes, and clever signs calling for the end of British imperialism and a reduction in air fares.

Despite these little incidents and a rare complaint from Actors Equity about non-payment of union dues, the gamey little bunch of troupers never forgot that the show must go on because there was really nothing else to do on this tacky sandspit.

They had tried other ways to pass the time until the

big Schubert rescue ship loomed large on the horizon.

Badminton.

Tuberculosis.

Treason.

Painting by numbers.

Lewd hand gestures.

The novelty always wore off, and each time they went back to *Porgy*. Undaunted by the nit-pickers who objected that the opera hadn't been written yet, they put on one helluva show at every performance. That was what was going on when that rum lot of gin-soaked Hollywood hacks and disbarred seamen blundered ashore. At the risk of sounding snobby, they were a lower class group; the kind who enjoy those big vulgar shows in Vegas with the topless showgirls and crude rat-tat-tat Brooklyn comics.

I'm not knocking Brooklyn.

George Gershwin himself was born there, and there's a bronze tablet on the house to say so.

But, Porgy and Bess was way over the head of that cheap package-tour crowd, so it's no wonder those goons thought it was a primitive tribal ceremony. The sloppy dancing didn't help, but after 8,736 performances any cast gets a bit stale.

There was a real communications problem.

Our sound system was lousy, so the gang from the ship couldn't hear clearly. They were also too bombed to see clearly, or they'd have realized that the cast was black— not Tahitian or Polynesian or anything like that. The cat who played Porgy had sung at Carnegie Hall; Bess had a Phi Bete key from Tuskeegee University, and the lead percussionist was an alumnus of the swinging Cab Calloway band.

58

Now get the picture.

Carl Denham—the producer—was half crazy with pain because his hat was too tight. He'd picked up someone else's in his panic to get off the ship, having tossed his cookies three or four times a day since the tramp freighter left New York.

Bruce Cabot was wild with excitement. Ann Darrow had promised to let him read his totally blank verse to her that night, and he figured that he might make out as she nodded off. Cabot was a lot trickier than he looked.

Not smarter though.

For the first nine days of shooting he thought it was a motorcycle picture. Absolute fact. He kept looking for Marlon Brando everywhere.

Ann Darrow—God bless her little mammaries—had a different problem. Near sighted. Kind to scorpions and senile Eskimos, but blind as a bat without contacts. Unfortunately, Dr. Rosenzweig hadn't invented them yet and she was too vain to wear conventional specs.

Marvelous kid.

Adored by the crew during every ridiculous picture she made—completely unspoiled.

Fabulous sense of smell (they develop that, you know).

Couldn't see six feet, but that wasn't a problem most of the time because how many people outside the circus have six feet?

She heard the music and the singing and the crowd, and she figured it was the Academy Awards. She'd always dreamt of an Oscar, yearned for the approval of her peers. She'd probably have had one years ago if she hadn't been so goddamn peerless. She deserved it.

The entire crew of nautical riff-raff was juiced to the gizzard, sluiced to the eyeballs and crocked to their hairline fractures. Captain Englehorn was not only tanked to the gills, but he had to go to the bathroom ... desperately.

Have you ever noticed that men with receding chins have weak kidneys and *Reader's Digest* stock? Englehorn was typical. Anyway, he was suffering and that always brought out the Prussian[14] accent he'd worked so hard to lose.

Englehorn sees[15] our Sportin' Life, and is so smashed he mistakes him for a tribal chief. The captain ignores the babbling of Denham, says nothing about coming in peace, and blurts out an urgent request for the shortest route to a toilet.

In a heavy *Prussian* accent.

"It's those buggers from the U-69!" our Sportin' Life warned his comrades in street talk that Englehorn couldn't understand

A classic cultural conflict, right?

That's how the whole mess began.

[14]See *Great Prussian Degenerates of the 20th Century* by Lenny Bruce (U. of Las Vegas Press), p. 88.

[15]I'll switch tenses any time I want, Nosey.

At this point, we should have gone to arbitration.

If the teachers and hospital workers unions can do it, why not actors, singers, dancers, musicians, sailors, movie folk, and prehistoric monsters?

If I'd been there, I would certainly have proposed *binding*[16] arbitration with the brontosaurus having the deciding tie-breaking vote.

In fact, I'd have insisted . . . and most people and enormous amphibians find my logic persuasive. Unfortunately, I was working on my math homework on the other side of the island. (A simple reflection of the tough quizzes that made our high school one of the top ten—up there with Andover, Exeter, Eton, Winchester, Laurel and Hardy. They really worked our tails off at Swamp High, something that bothered the reptiles a lot but didn't trouble me because 132-foot apes don't have tails. Don't get much either.

That's why I went into therapy.

We'll catch that later. It isn't as if I didn't have some fine chances with a couple of sea monster sisters, but I was kind of shy and they swam away sadly. One of them's doing a single up at Loch Ness in Scotland, and the other currently represents Atlantis at the United Nations.)

[16]*My Creepy Life* by the Marquis de Sade (Sickee Books), p. minus 24.

Going back to my situation when the movie mob arrived, I was the designated valedictorian of my graduat-
ing class and had just been notified that I would receive
the Frankenstein Medal for Geometry and Mass De-
struction. My trig was simply fantastic, and I was—if
you'll pardon the expression—very big in extracurricular
activities. I was captain of the debating team, co-chair-
man of the choir, and vice-president of the Young Con-
servatives Club. I was always great at tests, and my
incredible scores in Polish and exorcism had just won me
"early admission" to Columbia College in New York City.

Yale and Southern Methodist had accepted me too,
but I was looking forward to the urban experience in a
sophisticated metropolis.

Here's a grabber for you, lover.

I was looking forward to visiting the Statue of Liberty
(a great looking chick and my size) and the *Empire State
Building!*

Ironic, huh?

You believe in predestination, ESP, or Peter Pan
Peanut Butter?

I do too.

How do you feel about artificial sweeteners and astrol-
ogy? No kidding. Me too, though I don't talk about it to
strangers.

I'm a Pisces, and we're known to be salacious, trust-
worthy, orthopedic, contrapuntal, and given to spitting
in the street. I eat a lot of fish, drink gallons of tartar
sauce, and breed piranha as a hobby.

Every monster should have a hobby.

I told that to Stalin once, but he sneered.

Maybe it was a belch.

He was so enigmatic, and terribly cheap. Do you think it's nice for the leader of a major power, a man who's respected as one of the most sadistic paranoids among the world's statesmen, to buy everything wholesale? Bargains, bargains, bargains . . . unbelievable.

Okay, I was getting ready for final exams when the trouble began on the other side of the island. It was one of those hot, sleepy, May days, so sultry that the pterodactyls who usually patrolled over the coast were drowsing in their cool cave. I was squaring isosceles triangles like child's play when the tragic confrontation occurred.

The language problem complicated things.

When the show folk shouted out the second chorus of those great lyrics, Englehorn was too ashamed to admit that he hadn't the foggiest.

"They're offering her to Kong!" he blurted.

Did you see that skinny kid?

Who the hell would take her?

First, let me state absolutely and flatly[17] that my total lack of interest in her wasn't for ethnic reasons. I am not prejudiced against any group—with the possible exception of the Rolling Stones. I often play tennis with Bill Cosby and never work on Duke Ellington's birthday. I haven't missed the opening of a new Martin Luther King High School in a decade. And I'm not one of those Beverly Hills liberals who talk a great game but send their kids to private schools. All my kids[19] are in public zoos, where they mix with everybody.

[17]Giant creatures tend to have foot problems.
[19]With the exception of one who scripts Clint Eastwood movies and another in a macrobiotic commune in New England.

There were several reasons why that girl didn't grab me.

First, ego.

I'm big enough to admit that I have an ego as big as that of Attila the Hun.

This girl was a reject. She'd already been offered to the hermaphrodactyl and Gen. Idi Amin and was turned down by both. Changing her hair style and dressing her up in a different color straw skirt didn't fool ol' Stan for a second . . . and I don't like seconds.

Nothing against the kid herself. She finally got her act together, devoted herself to the public interest, and now heads the ladies' toilet division of the Department of Health, Education, and Welfare in Washington. Even though she never learned to type, she was deeply caring and had a warm way with people and wholesale plumbing firms.

Second, self-preservation.

When you grow up in a jungle ghetto like I did (okay, *as* I did) you develop a certain shrewdness. You heard of street smarts? Nothing compared to jungle smarts.

That jungle was a jungle, with terrible drainage. We had mosquitoes four feet long—every one of them a misfit. We appealed to the League of Nations, the League of Women Voters, and the National Football League for help.[37] We also sent a postcard pleading for the Duchess of Kent to intervene with the king, or at least to tamper with him a bit. All we got from her was a crudely-knit

[37]The League of Nations sent us a photo of Emperor Haile Selassie, the Women Voters mailed a questionnaire to be filled out, and the NFL sued us in a federal court in Omaha.

scarf[42] of scratchy wool for "aged almoners." Heed this lesson, Jack (queline). Street creatures have to make it on their own.

Look out for Number One—and don't trust Numbers Eight through Nineteen, either.

That girl was a plant.

A rhododendron, I think. Or was it dracaena? I don't know exactly, but several of her best friends were Venus Fly Traps.[26]

That girl wasn't half as innocent as she looked . . . or nearly as old. Let me spell it out for you.

J . . . a . . . i . . . l . . . B . . . a . . . i . . . t.

You dig?

San Quentin Quail.

Mess around with an underage female, and you're off to Sing Sing or the Tower of London for a very fast three to five years in the leather-working shop. Belts, saddles, and an occasional whip for those S–M shoppes that are always having sales on chains and handcuffs. Not for this ole ape, no siree.

There was a fourth reason that I'm a bit reluctant to go into after all these years. After all, she's a respected civil servant and teaches Sunday School to addicted Girl Scouts in the Inner City. (That's an all-night dry cleaners, I believe.) If my political opponents hadn't made this a campaign issue and hadn't spread scurrilous prefabrications from Formosa, I'd be prepared to let sleeping teen-agers lie. They do a great deal of it rather naturally.

[42]The brontosaurus still wears it regularly on Agatha Christie's birthday.

[26]You have a filthy mind, and should save your money for treatment.

Truth is my bag, Doc.

That's always been the Kong family credo.

The plain unvarnished truth (knotty pine is our most popular model) is that her reputation was none too good. Her personal hygiene was worse; even the mosquitoes stayed away from Sandra. I won't mention her last name, since I never hold a grudge.[15-1/2] She's married to a deacon and has five violent children. Those who know the family confide that their formative years were difficult, largely because their father selfishly refused to beat them, turn alcoholic, or abandon the mother for some floozy.

Looking backward is often painful.

You can easily get a stiff neck, or a funny chalky taste in your mouth.

Let's wrap up that first meeting by saying that there was a good deal of misunderstanding, confusion, and poor taste shown by all concerned.

The smartest thing that Englehorn and Denham ever did—before, during, and after this movie—was to take Ann Darrow back to the ship.

They should have left her there.

[15-1/2]I can hold my breath for nine minutes and forty seconds, which can be handy when you're near people like Sandra.

Maybe you don't remember all the details.

After all, you're a very busy person between your job, your family, your coded reports to a certain government agency, and that mad whirl of cocktail parties, petty thefts, and extramarital escapades.

Please, go in for a checkup.

You can't be too careful, even if you're in the prime, the pink, the red white and blue, and good graces of the Mafia. (Of course we really know that there is no Mafia, but just a lot of trashy innuendoes by jealous Chinese restaurant owners embittered by the success of pizza parlors.)

So to recap the details, the yo-yo took Ann Darrow back to the ship when bumbling Englehorn told producer Carl Denham that the "wild natives" had been planning to offer the teen tootsie (Sandra Sweaty) to one Kong as a sacrifice.

"You can't come in without tickets," was what was actually said.

"Can we use the bathroom?" blurted Englehorn.

"No, and you can't use the phone either unless you get up eight-eighty apiece."

"For a touring company? You must be out of your gourd."

"We don't take gourds, but you can pay in cheddar cheese or ball-point pens."

"You're all bananas," Englehorn fenced in his pidgin polyglot.

"We don't take bananas either. If the blonde can sew, we'll take her. Our costume and wardrobe mistress is all knotted up with rheumatic acne."

From that direct and simple conversation, kidney-crazed Captain Englehorn drunkenly brewed up his cockamamie yarn that the *Porgy* troupe wanted to swap six local ladies for Ann Darrow. On that idiotic note, the landing party went back to the *Venture* for a light brunch of luke-warm Canadian sherry, monosodium glutamate, and the stale fortune cookies carried in the hold as ballast.

The creator of this hideous cuisine was supposedly a skilled Chinese cook—in reality an undercover operative for Chiang Kai-shek. The only person on the vessel who knew this was Englehorn, crack Nazi agent who reported directly to Heinrich Himmler in Berlin via a radio concealed in his electric pencil sharpener. Himmler—sworn enemy of Marlene Dietrich, Albert Einstein, and Dr. Frankenstein—was convinced that the crew of the U-69 was being held captive on the island.

Chiang's spy was on the boat trying to find Dr. Frankenstein's secret laboratory. How could Chiang have known in 1932, you ask, that Universal Pictures would be sold and its stock would go right through the roof? Simple. The seer who made all those incredible predictions for the fortune cookies had read the future and warned Chiang that an army of irresistible humanoid agents and producers was being readied in Dr. Frankenstein's lab for world conquest. Dr. Frankenstein, a great humanitarian and lens expert, had left the island months earlier to donate all his discoveries and patents to the U.S. War

Department which gratefully misfiled every one of them. They were discovered in 1947, and today America has the finest force of humanoid bureaucrats in the Free World.

There's one more secret that can now be revealed—at last.

Also for the first time.

Bruce Cabot was more than met the eye. J. Edgar Hoover had personally selected him—picked him over Pat O'Brien and Bing Crosby—to make this journey into the unknown.

Never convinced that the corpse in Red Square in Moscow actually was Nikolai Lenin, the patriotic head of the FBI sent Bruce Cabot to check out a report that the supposed film company was furtively carrying weapons to Lenin—still conspiring devilishly at a secret Commie base.

"That body in Moscow may not be Lenin," Hoover whispered when Cabot met him in the closely-guarded FBI sauna somewhere in Washington?"

"Who's Lenin?"

"Very good. Play dumb, Cabot, and look out for those Commie rats who may be conspiring devilishly. If they break your cover or your kneecaps, call collect."

"Person to person, J. E.?"

"Only after nine o'clock. Night rates are cheaper."

Cabot considered this carefully.

"Suppose I don't find the Commie rats, sir?" he inquired respectfully.

"Well, we could always use a tall forward for the FBI basketball team. Keep your eyes open. You'll trip less often."

It was touching to think that J. Edgar Hoover, one of the shortest and most graceful[86] men in North America, worried about Cabot's dry-cleaning bills.

"How will I keep in touch, Chief?"

Hoover handed him a cage of carrier pigeons and a boot in the ass before vanishing into the vapor, leaving Cabot with a warm feeling and a nasty bruise.

Was it George Burns or Gracie Allen who said that "The best laid schemes o' mice and men Gang aft a'gley" . . . and what the hell did it mean? The plans of Mr. Hoover—known as "The Director" to the boys at the Bureau and the girls at the Chez Paree—usually worked, but this time the bungling of meddlers and the meddling of bunglers combined to gang them a'gley. Actually it wasn't the plans that ganged but the pigeons. Captain Englehorn, vicious Nazi that he was, found the carrier pigeons in the cage. Fed up with the horrible Chinese food, Englehorn baked the birds in a sauerkraut casserole and ate them all. . . .

He ate the casserole too. . . .

That's a Nazi for you.

Let's get back to the ship.

All was not lost, for the wily J. Edgar Hoover had a Plan B ready in case Cousin Brucie screwed up. I believe that he expected Brucie to blow it somehow, and was really using Cabot as a decoy, a diversion. The enemy agents were supposed to spot him, while the main U.S. undercover operative would go undetected.

Who?

[86]The 1924 polka champion of San Antonio, Texas—middleweight division.

Ann Darrow, of course.

With that body and hair-do, who'd suspect her of being America's most fatale femme in the annals of cloak, suit, and dagger history? Yes, it was innocent looking Col. Ann Darrow—highest ranking woman in the U.S. Marine Corps—who led the search for Nikolai Lenin and his Commie Rat Five. She had all their records . . . and perfect pitch. Her transmitter was cleverly hidden in an enema bag, which required her to fake frequent gastric problems. Of course the vile parody of the elegant Mandarin cuisine that she endured daily—for her country and her brother in the home—made regular communication with the FBI in Hawaii easier.

She radioed in every twenty-four hours.

Everything was going well until the stage manager of the *Porgy* troupe came out to the ship that night to offer her a job. She wasn't kidnapped. No siree. She jumped at the chance to get off that tub and see whether Nikolai Lenin and his band were anywhere on the island.

Cabot, Englehorn, and Denham all misunderstood.

They usually did.

They jumped to the bizarre conclusion that she was going to be sacrificed to Kong, and without the foggiest idea that Kong was the top math scholar on Zumdum, they took up arms. . . . Also legs, teeth, and repeating rifles.

They hurried ashore looking for Ann and trouble.

They found both.

Such a headache—I'll never forget it.

Almost like those migraines.

I was asleep on the other side of the big swamp, where the Holiday Inn is now. I'd put in a hard night pounding the old books—and 240 pounds of shark I was going to flatten for scallopini—and I was in a deep slumber. More precisely, I was in my huge duplex-cave snoring—slow asleep. I've always been a slow sleeper. The sleeping you can handle in seven hours takes me ten. According to Mom, this kind of thing walks in the family.

Let's get back to the headache.

Bang! Bang! Bang!

The guy who used to play with Cab Calloway (lacrosse, I think) was kicking the gong around . . . with a club. (According to my diary[77] it was the New York Athletic Club, but the RKO files claim it was the Yale Club. Whom are you going to believe, a big, good-natured ape with a global reputation for integrity and violence or those silk-shirted hype artists who did public relations for a money-grubbing[78] Hollywood outfit?

No contest, right?)

I put up with the noise for about ten minutes, but then

[77]Unpublished manuscript on deposit at the Library of Congress. Any offers?

[78]In contrast with today's socially responsible and artistic movie companies who might well need a 132-foot gorilla with a flair for sophisticated comedy.

I'd had it ... up to here. No, look higher. So I did what
any law-abiding prehistoric monster[49] would do; I called
the police.

They didn't come, and that didn't surprise me.

For several reasons.

First, everyone knows that you can never find a gen-
darme when you need one. Jean Valjean did a whole
book[126] on the subject, which sold very well at small
liberal arts colleges even if it was suppressed by the de
Gaulle government for poor binding.

Second, phone service was never adequate on Zumdum
—a tropical backwater ignored by the frontwaters, tidal
eddies, and crashing breakers who dominate Amagansett,
Santa Barbara, Virginia Beach, and the Postal Service
of Great Britain.

To oversimplify the problem, we had no phones on the
island. Lots of booths, but no phones. We did receive
bills every month. Whenever we didn't pay promptly they
installed more booths to get even. That phone company
was extremely even—you could say symmetrical—in the
fair way it clobbered everyone. Of course, monopolies
are like that. I learned that as a kid from my fourth grade
ski instructor, Mr. Lenin.[2,605] He always urged us kids to

[49]"Monster" is a pejorative term, a racial slur that must be
stamped out of popular usage in a democratic society. It's all
subjective. One man's monster is another's orthopedist and a
third's sister-in-law. Knock it off.

[126]Under the pseudonym of Victor Hugo, to avoid being
hassled by laws and orders. See *My Sewer*—winner of the 1911
Prix des Cochons Sacrés.

[2,605]A kind but strange bearded chap who often entertained
us by singing "The Internationale" and "Fly Me to the Moon."
He had a dog named Engels and a fondness for cringing at loud
noises.

shout to each other—across ravines and dangerous swamps—to screw the monopoly out of the dimes. Lenny, as we creatures called him, never told us what dimes were, and nobody asked because we didn't want to break his heart.

We'd already broken his collarbone and left leg several times. Giant creatures will be giant creatures, as Dr. Spock wrote in his masterful study[8] of family relations. Oh yes, there was another reason why the police didn't come. The nearest station house was about 700 miles away, as the pterodactyl flies.

Bang! Bang! Bang!

I listened to the music, regretfully noted that it didn't sound Latin (N.B. I've always wanted to visit Puerto Rico.) and decided to go down to say a few well-chosen words to the inconsiderate merrymakers.

I was furious, and not a wee bit worried that I might not come up with the well-chosen words. Today, my good and trusty friend Wally[2.4] helps me out with special material but our paths and mutually myopic glances hadn't crossed then so I was a trifle edgy. I knew plenty of words. Fish, whistle, bravo, kill . . . and dozens more. The problem was selecting the right ones. My adjectives were first-rate, but the adverbs weren't up to Ivy League[68] standards. As I smashed aside trees and shattered bould-

[8]Later novelized so adroitly by Mario Puzo as *The Godfather*.

[2.4]For a brief and entirely false account of how this warm but shallow friendship began, and why Mr. Kong asked Mr. Wally Wager to help with this manuscript, please see the introduction.

[68]I've come far since those days; last September my gerunds were admitted to the freshman class at Princeton . . . on a full scholarship.

ers, I went through my glossary to choose my words well.

I must have known, somehow, that what I was going to say would be recorded for posterity (a wholly owned subsidiary of RKO). The noise was getting louder and louder and louder as I drew nearer and nearer and nearer . . . and nearer. It wasn't just that gong anymore. Those weirdos were playing and singing at the top of their gall bladders. It wasn't anything from *Porgy and Bess*.

I was stunned.

Also very angry.

"What the hell are you nuts doing?" I asked politely in a voice that cracked dishes on Guam.

"You love it, don't you?"

"Not really," I said truthfully. "It isn't Gershwin, is it?"

He shook his little beady head shyly.

I was impressed by the resemblance to a black Woody Allen.

"No, Mr. Kong, it's the opening number of the second act of *Showboat*. Music by Jerome Kern, lyrics by Oscar Hammerstein the Second. Neat, huh?"

I was in a tough spot. Hammerstein was a Columbia grad and I was going there in a couple of months, and the code of the Sapersteins is that loyalty is next to godliness.

"Why no more *Porgy?*" I tap-danced evasively.

"Can't do Gershwin all the time. It's a great new world out there, Mr. Kong. Lots of people writing wonderful stuff. Mark my words, Mr. Kong, this Hammerstein's going to write *The King and I* and *South Pacific* with a sharp young kid named Richard Rodgers, and they're going all the way."

I wasn't taking any chances, and I wasn't paying any attention to the undernourished chick in the cheap blond wig either.

"Where did Rodgers go to school?" I fenced as I counted the hairs on her left leg.

"Columbia!"

I smiled, and Ann Darrow let out a holler that could arouse Dracula.[472] When I think about it—usually when my gums smart—I can understand why. I didn't look too great. I was right in the middle of $4,300 worth of orthodontistry, and my chops were not in great shape. I didn't normally look anything like this. I certainly didn't usually go out at night just in a fur jock, but that's something we'll go into later. (I can say that fashion has never meant a lot to me, which is more than Elton John or Elizabeth Taylor can say.)

So my teeth were a bit of a mess and my hair wasn't combed and I wasn't really dressed for meeting people, but I was annoyed and that counts for something. That hysterical Ann Darrow was screaming and moaning in a manner that was definitely seductive . . . at least to a kid who wasn't even twenty yet. Her act was highly suggestive, but I still had the headache and I couldn't be quite sure what she was suggesting.

Tennis?

A potato race?

Perhaps a potato knish and a roll in the hay? (Or was it a hay knish and a roll in the potatoes?)

Embarrassed by my own adolescent naiveté, I decided to pick her up. The brontosaurus had told me that pick-

[472]Years later, I used to play poker every Friday night with Dracula, Peter Lorre, Boris Karloff, and a tough cookie from Warner Brothers who usually won. Dracula was a poor poker player, a good loser, and only so-so as a vampire. Never bit nuns or war wounded, though.

ups could be fun and lead to some far-out action. Not being sure exactly what he meant because my vocabulary, glossary, and aviary were limited, I picked up Ann Darrow and took her off to discuss the matter further in private. That was the name of my cave, private.

I must admit that I also had something else in mind. I'd eaten a large octopus for dinner and still had bits stuck in my choppers. I thought that this skinny broad might make a good toothpick. I certainly never had any idea of making the doll herself. One look told me that she was a married woman, virtuous, and probably frigid.

As I turned away from her, there were four things I didn't know.

First, why was she there. The music director made that clear at once.

"So we're square now?" he shouted from the wall.

He was settling my refund claim for seats with obstructed vision by paying with Ann Darrow. I had no idea what she was worth, but I'd take her if they'd stop all the noise.

"Okay—if you knock off the *Showboat* stuff," I agreed.

"How about a medley of Verdi's greatest hits?"

That was too much, so I beat on my chest to let him know that enough was enough. (You can't be nice to show folk. They're all animals.)

Now the second thing I didn't know was that the RKO phonies were up on the wall, filming madly. I'd never heard of RKO, the BBC, or even the FBI.

And that brings me swiftly to the fourth item. Neither I nor the thespians nor the RKO contingent suspected what Ann Darrow had in mind.

She *wanted* me to carry her off into the steamy jungle,

77

across the fetid swamp to my luxurious cave with that breath-taking view of the quicksand. Those were her orders. Search every nook and cranny, adam and eve, sundae and malted to find out whether Nikolai Lenin and his Commie Rats may be lurking, smirking, or jerking there.

You just didn't horse around with J. Edgar.

Off we went, me and the skinny woman in that tacky blond "rug." Looked like a scalp left over from a low-budget picture about Custer's last juice stand. Ann Darrow shrieking into my ear, making my headache worse. (Also my right foot hurt because I wasn't wearing my arch-support loafers.) I could hear the movie morons crashing along behind me in tepid pursuit. What the hell were we all doing out here at 4:10 in the morning, I wondered. We could get mugged.

There is no way—*no way at all*—that anyone can hold me responsible for what happened to those dumb Boy Scouts who chased after me into the dangers of that dark and poorly-drained jungle. It wasn't my idea. I'd never met them, and Mom taught me never to play squat tag with strangers during the hay fever season.

If anybody should know, it ought to be Merian Cooper.

After all, the whole picture was his idea and he did the basic treatment.

Would you be surprised to learn that when I asked him about this in 1971, he feigned ignorance and hit a deadly lob that nicked the baseline—which shattered into a hundred pieces.

"Wasn't my idea, Stan. How about double or nothing... an even oxhead of chablis?"

Why would I take such a sucker bet?

I didn't even own an ox.

78

Then I asked Bruce Cabot, whose savvy, Sephardic broker had advised him into a tremendous killing in Babylonian War Bonds. Cabot was now living very comfortably on his immense avocado ranch in downtown Boston.

"Chablis?" he said. "How disgusting!"

"Was it you, Bruce? Level with me."

He thought hard, shrugged, and dramatically adjusted his underclothes.

"I think it was Mel Brooks, King."

"You dummy. Mel Brooks wasn't even in that picture."

Always eager to please, he offered me an autographed avocado and did his ever popular impression of Mary Martin. Who could stay mad at a mug like that?

Finally, I had a hunch. It was a 48 long—a bit snug but nice stitching. One thing you learn in Hollywood is to trust your instincts. (God knows you can't trust anyone or anything else.) My first instinct was to give up the whole search and go back to complete my cello concerto, but my second prevailed.

Englehorn!

Mad dog, Nazi, mother-grabber, and spy-killer–saboteur.

It wasn't easy to find him—he'd had plastic surgery that completely changed his footprints—but through certain connections in the Pentagon—individuals who remember what I did on classified missions behind the Wehrmacht lines during World War II—I tracked Englehorn down to a moated castle in southern Spain where he was living even better than Bruce Cabot. No avocados, but swell oranges and some great tomatoes.[89]

"The game is up, Herr Englehorn!"

[89]Including two sisters named Maria and Lupe.

"You're Israeli, aren't you? I knew you'd come sooner or later, and I'm tired of running."

"Run much?"

"No, but I jog a lot. Can't we make a deal? I'll tell you about the others, and I'll throw in some obscene Dürer engravings that will knock your fillings out."

I tried to feel sorry for him, but I couldn't.

"I'm half-Philadelphian, you Nazi swine, and Philadelphians don't make deals."

"How about half a deal?" he begged.

Now what the hell could I do with half a deal?

"How about the truth on who sent those poor sailors out to die in that teeming jungle?"

He began to sob.

He wasn't too bad at it either; I've seen Bruce Cabot do a lot worse.

Then he made a desperate lunge for a Luger in the drawer of his desk, which I adroitly pulped into tinder.

"What happened to my hand?" he screamed in unbearable agony as he withdrew his hand from the pile of tinder that used to be a desk.

"Riddles bore me. Who was responsible, punk?"

After I twirled him up and down the chimney a few times to clean the flue, he admitted that he was the one who'd given the fatal orders.

" 'Follow that giant ape! There's an extra ten bucks if you don't lose him.' That's what I told them," he confessed.

It was as if a huge burden—or some bad stomach gas—had lifted. I'd been blaming myself for all those victims, and now I felt better. I tossed Englehorn out of the third-floor window and into the arms of the nine waiting Israeli agents. If you think literary agents can be rough, you ought to see what that Tel Aviv group did to him as they dragged him off to long-overdue[555] justice.

Okay, I took off with Ann Darrow screaming directions in my ear, making a complete ass of herself because she knew nothing of the local roads or traffic. The ship's crew and the ambitious movie producer chased after me, and if they got into trouble out there in No Man's Land[512] it wasn't my fault.

Still, the fates that they met were terrible.

Remember?

[555]The best kind.
[512]Great for monsters, though.

She didn't stop hollering for a second.

"Look out for the python . . . take a left at the cesspool . . . low dinosaur ahead."

Nag, nag, nag . . . and *loud*.

I should have suspected that there was a method to her badness; she was making all that noise to cover the sounds of the gang chasing us. I was just a twenty-year-old super-ape, unfamiliar with worldly women and diuretics. Who could guess that this dippy blonde was one of the bravest, most resolute and incompetent secret operatives in the history of organized sports in America?

On and on we trekked, through neighborhoods where even the brontosauruses won't go alone. Tough? You wouldn't believe it, and she kept screaming.

"Slow down . . . you've missed your turn . . . don't tailgate that tyrannosaurus, he's drunk."

With that uproar, I didn't hear my dog approaching through the clotted underbrush. What dog? You don't recall any dog, do you? Fess up. Why should you? Those picture guys gave you a lot of trick photography. Remember that part where they were trotting along after me and, all of a big fat sudden, a dinosaur steps into the frame and does two choruses of "Stormy Weather"? That was my dog.

Would I kid you, a true believer?

That was Paul, very affectionate.

He was an Alsatian retriever—the only breed that could

survive on Zumdum. Cockers, poodles, Canadian hairless, and Mexican boxers[43b] just couldn't cut the mustard in that climate, but Alsatian retrievers stuck to chili sauce and took it all in stride. The Alsatian retriever is a rather large dog—slightly bigger than a school bus—and its average stride is about eighteen and a half feet. Sometimes it uses smaller strides of only fifteen inches, but then it trips a lot. On Alsatian national holidays, it doesn't stride at all but stays home and gets disgustingly drunk . . . in traditional folk costume.

The breed is not without its problems. First, it will not retrieve grouse, trees, or lost Hondas. The only thing an Alsatian retriever will retrieve is Alsatians. It's terrific at that. If there's an Alsatian within ninety miles—even a small one—it will find and retrieve. Second, this breed still is imbued with the Protestant work ethic and can't stand fooling around. Committed to an honest day's work, it gets rather grumpy when there aren't any Alsatians to retrieve.

The night those yo-yos came chasing after me through the jungle was the end of Bock Day. Named to honor the birthday of Alexandre Graham Bock, the inventor of dark beer and statutory rape, Bock Day is Alsace's greatest feast. Back in Strasbourg, overweight and red-faced Alsatians usually celebrate by painting graffiti on their goats, molesting minors, munching peppery wursts stuffed with nails to symbolize the expulsion of the Mongols in 1211, and drinking great steins of dark beer until their kidneys back up and they go temporarily deaf. That's what my dog did, and that's why Paul was bombed out of his skull

----

[43b]Not so the wrestlers, who swept the league.

when the "rescue party" came brushing through the undercharge.[455]

They saw Paul wallowing around in his colorful costume. Being terribly provincial, they mistook his quaint outfit, and being scared, they jumped to the conclusion that he was a brontosaurus. They were simple lads, over their depth and out of their gourds. . . . Which was hardly surprising, since they were a short group of very modest depth.

Let's be fair. All the blame shouldn't be dumped on their round shoulders. Being intoxicated and grumpy and longing desperately to get in a good retrieve, Paul carelessly concluded that they were Alsatians.. They smelled funny, a bit like over-ripe Alsatians. He couldn't hear them shouting in fractured English . . . he was temporarily deaf in the wonderful old tradition.

Paul, big playful puppy, came bounding to retrieve them, and those dumb mothers shot him. They also gassed him, as I recall, and kicked him in a very tender place. He didn't mind that so much; it was a beloved part of the Alsatian yuletide celebration to boot and hammer friends and family in such spots. He let out a couple of hearty laughs to show that he was a good sport, and then they shot him some more and pulled his tail.

On and on Bruce Cabot & Co. plunged and plunged, right into the swamp. They were, of course, unprepared for the rigors. They had neither longboats nor shortboats, and there wasn't a kayak, canoe, or cabin cruiser in the crowd. They also carried the wrong lenses, which ac-

[455]Overcharging is actually much more common during the rest of the year, especially in months ending with epidemics.

counts for the poor quality of the film they shot that night. The darkness was filled with the horrid sounds of mosquito squadrons circling for the kill, and Cabot's mind was full of mush. Carl Denham's skull was buzzing with fear—the kind movie producer's feel when they sense overtime lurking in the next bush.

"Let's build a raft to cross the swamp," somebody said.

I doubt it was Cabot. . . .

He didn't speak in such long sentences.

They built a crude raft rather crudely, and started poling their way across the murky waters through the murky fog. Because the fog was so murky, they couldn't see too good and somehow didn't notice the slobosaurus rising from the murk. That should give you some idea of the sort of meatballs RKO hired for this flick.

Have you ever seen a slobosaurus?

They're hard not to notice.

About 225 feet long, close to 40 feet high, and pointy earlobes you don't easily forget.

They don't look much like a fish-and-chips stand or a roadside billboard for Johnny Walker Red.

No one with an IQ over sixty could not notice a slobosaurus, but these idiots completely missed it. He gave them the old double-reverse that Notre Dame used so effectively against Sandhurst, William and Mary, and Marks and Spencer in the Rose Bowl. He belly-dived, came up, and blitzed the raft. I believe they call it red-dogging now . . . or is it eating an ineligible receiver?

If they'd kept their heads, they might have worked something out. Slobosauruses are always willing to bargain. However, the RKO bunch started screaming and puking and the slobosaurus kept its head. When the

85

survivors made all that noise and ran away pell-mell, lickety-split, and Big Mac, that got up his appetite and he lumbered after them in luke-warm pursuit. (With the temperature in the nineties, it was much too steamy for hot pursuit.)

Anyway, I was shambling-ambling-rambling along Interstate 96 heading home with a yawn in my face and a dizzy blonde in my mitt. She kept whispering things in my ear—things that made me blush. (You would not believe the far-out ideas she had. Guess those show folk are all degraded at heart, at least late at night.) Suddenly I heard something behind me, and I looked back wearily.

Not again.

That dumb slobosaurus was staggering all over the jungle, crashing into trees, ruining property values, and whistling way off key. It just wasn't my night.

"Hang on, Toots," I said as I parked her on a tree stump. "Gotta go make a citizen's arrest."

Still feeling some affection for the slobosaurus' sister whom I'd known—in the Biblical sense, I'd brought him home several times before—I started back, a bit bleary eyed because I'd forgotten to put in my contacts when that damn gong woke me up.

I was not stoned.

Unlike a lot of other very big stars, I've stuck to the old-fashioned ways and morals of my foremothers and I never smoked stones.

A little gravel, yes—but only once in a while.

I was simply tired, and a bit rattled by the dame's daring dialogue that had dilated my capillaries and scorched my earlobe.

When I got to that large tree across the ravine, I saw

something moving on it. Lots of small scurrying things—
and that got me mad.

Also a trifle scared.

I thought they were roaches. In that dim light, in that
murky jungle—me without my glasses—they looked a lot
like roaches.

"There goes the neighborhood," I thought. Somebody
must have left the gate in the wall ajar, or maybe the gate-
keeper had a couple of jars of Bushmills himself. Whatever, I didn't hesitate to do my duty as I seen it. I flipped
those "roaches" into the ravine, and went back to the
blonde.

Big surprise....

She was in trouble.

That staggering slobosaurus had tottered into the
clearing, running two traffic lights and the 1,000-meter
dash in a dreary seven minutes flat. He made a crude pass
at Ann Darrow.

"Go home, Bert," I said as I jovially shattered one of
his eardrums with a fraternal punch. "Go home. You're
making a fool of yourself in front of strangers."

He turned ugly (a very short trip for a slobosaurus).
He insulted my mother, trampled my gardenia garden,
and ruined my hairdo with a left jab. I beat the hell out
of him, beat my wonderful chest, and then just beat it.
I jogged on to the cave, unaware that Bruce Cabot was
doggedly dogging my footsteps.

I said it before and I'll say it again.

It just wasn't my night.

Everything possible had gone wrong, and things were
going to get worse.

The way they filmed my cave was an absolute disgrace, and certainly did nothing to improve property values in the neighborhood. As a matter of fact, after the picture played on the island—on a double-bill with *Rape of the Zombies*—two families of scorpions and a nice old couple of retired hair dressers moved to an abandoned coal mine where the carbon monoxide concentrations were high but security was better.

The movie crowd made my swinging bachelor pad look like a dump. Well, to paraphrase a certain pouch-faced patriot who did a lot for the tape-recorder business and the pardon industry—my home was not a dump. True, it had once been a garbage heap where the dinosaurs tossed their gnawed carcasses and, after parties, their cookies, but never a dump. At worst, a septic tank.

That had been during the Evolutionary War when Our Crowd[78] fought to drive out the British hairy mammoths who wanted to tax T . . . and also F and R. (The local creatures felt this was both unreasonable and contrapuntal; they did use F a bit, but rarely T and R. They were already paying a stiff excise on imported vowels, towels, and musket balls.)

Let's get the facts straight.

I owned my flat—a spacious duplex with a terrific view. It was a condominium that set me back a large bundle of

[78]Including several Unitarians.

bananas, air-conditioned and equipped with all modern conveniences including closed circuit TV, a leprous door-man, and parking in the basement. Actors, hookers, rock stars, and tax accountants weren't allowed to buy into the place, and amoebic infections were also excluded. One of the Left Wing newspapers in Calcutta—a lively weekly named *KILL!*—has falsely charged that Indians were barred from the premises.

Another bloody tissue of falsehoods.

(Kleenex, I think.)

I myself had a sleep-in Sioux butler for years, and a nicer chap you couldn't find.[5¼] I gave him twenty pounds and a warm embrace when he left on a football scholar-ship to play for the Royal Academy of Dramatic Arts in London, and I hear that he's now chief designer of pros-thetic devices for the Tate Gallery.

What about Pakistanis, you ask.

Why?

What the hell have Pakistanis got to do with my high-class high rise? They're a wonderful people, and if I ever meet one[98.6] I'll tell him/her so. Please get your head together and try to concentrate on my quarters. They were swell, better than that fleabag where you live.

The movie crowd deliberately used a dirty lens to make my place look crummy. As for that snake, I never saw him before in my life. (Not Ann Darrow, dummy—the creepy serpent you saw attack me in the garage when I brought Ann Darrow home to see my etchings.)

[5¼]He was especially hard to find on General Custer's birth-day.

[98.6]Or two, or even four.

89

Try to remember. It was a long, nasty serpent, a real tricky fighter. I was telling Ann Darrow this terrific story —a teensy weensy bit smutty—when this snake jumped me without warning or provocation. I figure that either the snake was a college friend of Bruce Cabot, a sailor in drag, or a paid tool of those tools at RKO. They probably brought that spaced-out snake with them, cheap cinema sensationalism of the worst sort.

Not that I look down on snakes. I went to school with some intelligent and affectionate cobras and a python who had a fantastic wiggle—really turned me on. I've fooled around with a snake or two in my time—just heavy petting—and I could introduce you to a lizard named Helen who knew numbers Xaviera Hollander couldn't imagine. However, I never messed with a *male* snake, and that's what this baby was.

"What do you think you're doing, Jack?" I hissed indignantly as he wrapped his cruddy coils about my noble frame.

"Hiissss!" he hissed back.

"You're crinkling my fur, Bud," I advised with a touch of impatience as he looped around my neck.

"Hiissss! Hiissss!" he hissed again in tones that communicated insolence and a fondness for garlic.

We'd never been introduced, and this sickie was trying to hustle me into an intimate personal relationship.

He was also trying to kill me—right in the middle of one of my best risque jokes. Undismayed, uncomfortable, and half undressed, I'm afraid I lost my cool. I hung onto my panache and Ann Darrow. . . . No, I put her down and picked up another panache and a velvet charisma that I'd won at bridge, and I slammed the stuffings out of that fresh serpent.

90

(Gorillas one, snakes nothing.)

Laughing jauntily and quoting clever lines from *Punch*, *The New Yorker*, and the State Unemployment Office, I wrapped the charisma about cute little Ann Darrow. She was like a child, happy and damp. I never found out whether it was perspiration in the jungle or weak kidneys.

There are a couple of other things I never found out.

Like what happened to my wallet?

Look, I'm not saying that an actress like Ann Darrow was a crook, and I refuse to put any credence in those rumors about what she did before she became a star. They make up stories like that about all the biggies—out of jealousy, I suppose. All I'm saying is that Ann Darrow got real friendly and cuddly, and sometime during those tender moments my wallet disappeared.

With all my credit cards, voter registration, and a photo of my mother in her darling waitress outfit. I have absolutely no proof that Ann Darrow stole my wallet. But if she didn't, who did? You can tell me now, Ann. I won't hold a grudge.

I can't say the same for the snake, one mean baby.

Okay, he wasn't quite a baby. He was about seventeen, which means that he could get a driver's license in a lot of states and, I think, Paraguay. It could be Uraguay, which my travel agent recommends highly. In any case, that snake wasn't an adult in my book (which sold very well, especially in campus bookstores).

I'm getting to the point. Don't shove.

I have always taken a very liberal position[55.5] on whatever consenting adults want to do. It's strictly okay with Big Stan, if you know what I mean. All these old-fash-

[55.5] See pp. 81—204 of the Kama Sutra.

ioned limitations seem pretty comical today, so I say different jokes for different folks and what the hell. (I have always been a great admirer of Elton John[711] and Michelangelo, and nobody can bad-mouth Oscar Wilde in my cave. You can be a bisexual, homosexual, soldier of fortune, or even a movie critic . . . all the same to this impartial and sophisticated observer.)

So why did I get sore at that snake?

First, he wasn't an adult.

Second, I never consented. I wasn't even asked. He wasn't asked either, and I can't stand trespassers, party crashers, or peanut-butter freaks traveling on Latvian passports. Several members of the British Labor Party have suggested that I used excessive force on that serpent, but that bleeding kidney liberal crap doesn't crush any ice cubes with this gorilla.

Do your own thing, but keep your coils off mine. . . .

Or at least ask.

Maybe send some candy and flowers, or a cashmere scarf. Fuschia would be nice.

Treat me courteously, and I'm a doll.

Fresh, and I hit. I once punched out the entire Barnard College field-hockey team—cute girls with knobby knees —for taking liberties with my person. (One of them landed up the Hudson River near Vassar College where she now teaches feminist philosophy and bicycle repair.)

Can't we get back to me and Ann Darrow?

After I simonized that snake, I took Ann Darrow upstairs. Need I mention that I didn't know (a) some nameless tart had stolen my wallet or (b) sneaky Bruce was

[711] A very talented man with atrocious taste in glasses.

creeping up behind us. It has always been his story that he was courageously trying to rescue his loved one from a fate worse than death, and that's the impression his buddies gave in the flick.

Merde!

(That's Austrian for dinosaur manure. Keep in mind that Mom's folks spoke Austrian pretty good for emigrants.)

Was Brucie really a hero, or perhaps a peeping Tom? I can't say and I'm not accusing him of any improprieties—except letting down the FBI when it was counting on him. I'm just wondering, and I'd love to know whether the sealed files of the Los Angeles Police Department might cast any light on his hobbies.

Any comments, Jack Webb? Ten-four... Adam-12?

Of course those giant studios can hush-up anything, people say. If Watergate had involved the head of a big film or TV outfit instead of that sweetie who wasn't a crook, we'd never have heard Word One. Does the press ever mention the connection between the boss of a major studio and that Santa Barbara water-ski repair firm that's wholly owned by the CIA, or ... never mind.

All I can say is that a lot of money was spent and a lot of strings pulled to fill the U.S. and foreign press with stories that your favorite author was just a thirteen-inch dummy filmed in miniature sets. Okay, I'm willing to discuss the height: 132 feet isn't exactly accurate; 131 feet 9½ inches in my stockinged paws is correct.

The dummy part is an absolute lie.

Ask those colleges that admitted me.

Still, my enormous contribution to that picture has been covered up and anybody who can cover up a 131-

foot-9½-inch gorilla is obviously a threat to a free press[222] and a well-informed American public.[82.06] If big-money interests can dominate the media and manipulate public opinion, it isn't just us giant apes who're in danger. You smaller monkeys are also in trouble, Buster (and Ms. Busterette).

Sure, there was some great stop-motion trick photography and a genius named Willis O'Brien made major contributions. You could say colonel contributions, for he was a wizard technical type,[1,417] and he also brought his own lunches to show loyalty. Still, those guys got all the publicity and cash and Stan Kong got shafted . . . also shot up a lot.

Now let's return to the scene up on the outdoor ledge and the sex bit—which was one of my favorites. Ann Darrow and I were up there enjoying the view on my terrace. It may have looked a bit naked because my butler had moved all the canvas furniture indoors when rain was forecast. (He'd also shifted the hibachi, which played a big part in some of my famous celebrity-packed barbecues.) It was a penthouse terrace, not a rocky ledge.

The rocks were in Cabot's head. Creeping up to sneak a look, he approached as I was getting to know Ann Darrow a bit better. There was a scene in the original film—cut out in 1938, I think, when the prurients took over—in which I peeled a few layers off Ann Darrow. Clothes, not skin. I did it because her garments were soaked, and I

[222]I myself never found a free press, and you wouldn't believe my dry-cleaning bills.

[82.06]You can provide your own joke here.

[1,417]About eighty words a minute.

wanted to get her out of those wet clothes and into one of my esteemed dry martinis.[2] I had no interest in her at all. Her appeal lay in her sincerity and tinkling laugh, and that one good cheekbone I mentioned earlier.

I have never told this to Ann Darrow, because she's a sensitive kid who vomits easily, but I wasn't turned on at all. In fact, I welcomed the noise of clumsy Cabot tripping over his hippie beads and took the noise as an excuse to split. It was while I was checking inside that the klepto-bird arrived.

Every department store and boutique in the swamp knew that poor sick pterodactyl, a compulsive shoplifter. With a wing span of about fifty feet, it had lifted quite a few shops and a couple of gas stations. Of course, its mother always made it return everything so there was really nothing for anyone to worry about. The bird couldn't possibly have any desire to munch on Ann Darrow; only a few hours earlier it had ploughed through a forty-one-course dinner including stuffing, cranberry sauce, and enough lemon meringue pie for a regiment of Coldstream Guards.

A petty, pathetic, pilferer came out a cannibal-rapist in that dirty movie, proving that filth is in the script of the beholder. I never got a chance to explain that to Ann Darrow, who was screaming her head off. (You can bet your ass that Jean Harlow wouldn't have cracked up like that.)

I've dealt with high-strung broads—and birds—before. I raced up to the terrace, gave the bird a swift rap in the

[2]Was this Bob Benchley's, Dorothy Parker's, or Howard Dietz's line?

chops, and then a chop in the raps. Ann Darrow's hollering caused the bird to panic, adding to the ridiculous confusion.

"I'll tell your father!" I warned the pterodactyl.

"O my God, he'll stop my allowance!" moaned the winged wacko.

While we were bickering, Cabot sneaked onto the terrace like a cheap cat-burglar and took off with Ann Darrow. The elevator wasn't good enough for those Hollywood snobs. They slipped out on a window-washer's rope —a routine that wasn't going to help my insurance premiums.

Did I note that Cabot was crazy jealous of Johnny Weissmuller, a strapping kid who was going good in a whole bunch of kid-pix about Tarzan? Consider it noted. Cabot envied all those adoring fans, mostly eleven-year-olds with nine-year-old IQs. Brucie had seen Johnny the Musclebound take quite a few dives, so, being a copycat, he talked Ann Darrow into trying the same bit. I think it fractured her wig and tore loose her expensive false navel.

She never saw my etchings—the Daumiers and one Rembrandt that the Met craved—but who cared? Thank heavens she's gone, I thought. I was tired and I had picked up a case[A] of the sniffles. I shrugged (a lot better than either Cabot or Weissmuller) and I mixed up a hogshead of my extra-dry martinis. After I'd sipped two or three gallons I felt better—but only for a moment.

My car keys were gone, and I had a damn good idea as to who'd pinched them.

[A]There's a ten-percent discount by the case.

96

Are there no limits to the baseness and grossness of those Hollywood barbarians who have vandalized our children's minds, raped a great art form, and really screwed up the beach at Malibu with those crappy houses that look like an ant colony in pickled pine and knotty money?

I have asked myself that question many times, often when suffering from constipation. It is a tough question, ranking up there with why were we put on this planet and does Jimmy Carter know more about treating psoriasis than Charlton Heston—who's very close to a number of divinities and plays one helluva game of tennis for his age.

At my age there's no point in beating around the bush. I believe—and this is just my personal conviction reached after much reflection, prayer, and suffering—that we were put on this planet because no other planet would have us. That isn't just humility. That's the polyester-pickin' truth.

Yes.

That's the answer to the second question.

Yes.

There are no limits to what those decadent movie and TV types will try to pull. They're rich, powerful, and spoiled—and I envy them plenty. However, I wasn't the least bit envious that morning when that baggage[m]

[m]Maybe I should say suitcase, which sounds better.

bugged out with my car keys leaving me stuck out there in the suburbs some six or seven miles from the nearest liquor store or supermarket. I was truly frosted, and that's why I took off after my Number One suspect.

Attention all barristers, solicitors,[q] attorneys, lawyers, counsel, magistrates, judges, J.P.s, feminists, and over-zealous[x] copy editors! I'm not saying that she swiped the keys, so don't get litigious or I'll sit on your court house. Maybe the butler did it, although that's unlikely since Indians are paragons of virtue and we really should return to them everything west of the Mississippi—including Ronald Reagan.[j] (I would hold back H. J. Deutchendorf, Jr.'s place at Aspen, because he's worked very hard for it and has a kind face.)

I could have lost the damn keys or maybe they fell into the crack of my splendid red-velvet couch. So let's just say that I couldn't find them, and I thought that it was just possible that she might have picked them up, mistaking them for one of her false earlobes. Hoping to discuss this with her in a civilized way and curious whether the *Porgy* troupe might be adding *Guys and Dolls* to their schedule, I made my way back to the wall.

Yes, I wasn't exactly strolling.

You might say[n] that I was bull-dozing along at top speed, wiping out enormous trees and rocks and anything else in the way. I was always impetuous, and the events that evening hadn't done much to improve my cool. The

[q]Except those on 8th Avenue in New York City.

[x]Is there any other kind?

[j]A man of principle and a credit to his race, the 440 high hurdles.

[n]Better not. I hate gossips.

last straw came as I neared the wall and found several roaches on *our* side—breeding like rabbits.[t] That dumb RKO crowd had let them through . . . accidentally, no doubt.

Then came the straw after the last straw.

(What's so impossible about that?

They sent someone out to buy more.)

They refused to let me in . . . *me*, a heavy investor in the show and a regular patron for more than 4,100 performances. I'd even helped them out and taken over one of the parts, and now this crap!

A deliberate slap in the face!

This . . . after my regular contributions to the civil rights movement, the Actors Fund, and the Motion Picture Industry Country Home for victims of the talkies?

Toooo much!

I began to rap on the door—a bit insistently.

They replied by shouting unspeakable (but shoutable) ethnic epithets, and they also threw gum wrappers, bicycle pumps, Czarist paper money (valueless and an insult to my emigrant ancestors—and my amigrant encestors too), empty suppository boxes, and crumpled publicity stills from *Godfather Two*.

My blood boiled, causing the wax in my ears to melt and run down onto my usually immaculate fur. I began banging on the door, pausing only now and then to thump my wonderful chest. The mob on the other side answered rudely with a medley of Palestine Liberation Organization marching songs and a few Vivaldi arias, irritating me even further.

Where the hell were my car keys?

[t]Same way gerbils and Albanians do it.

"Toss them over the wall and I'll forget the whole thing," I offered with characteristic generosity.

The only reply was two choruses of Handel's *Messiah*—in the wrong key.

I put my splendid shoulder into the door, which popped open like a stale croissant—showering the punks inside with rotted timbers and some sesame seeds. At this moment, all those midgets inside were screaming and belching and tripping over their feet and roaches. I could clearly recall my mother's voice.

"Schmutzig! Schmutzig!"

The ingrates began to run. I wasn't feeling too well. I didn't know why, but it was my own fault. I took a deep breath, inhaled two sailors and a soprano, and charged in to find my keys. I had no fear in charging, being unaware that my credit cards were gone. Despite the impression you got from the film, not all the comments made were negative.

"Fine looking chap."

"Damn graceful, isn't he?"

"Who's his agent? He's a natural!"

Those are only a few that I clearly recall.

Well, not so clearly.

I was feeling a bit fuzzy, but maybe that was because I was five weeks overdue at the barber.[8q] Now I caught a glimpse of that schlocky blonde wig, and I headed straight for it.

[8q]I was his biggest customer, so his business collapsed when I left and he went to Philly to try his luck as a composer. He punched out a couple of nifty choral works and symphonies, and picked up a Pulitzer Prize. I wish I had his talent—and his wonderful friends.

That's when those goons fired the gas bombs.

Why?

I already had gas, and a funny head. I staggered for a second, but only because I'd stepped in some roach doo. Then I felt woozy, and it suddenly hit me. Coricidin! I'd taken a pawful for the sniffles, forgetting that you weren't supposed to drink booze with antihistamines. The combination of those martinis and the Coricidin really clobbered me, and I slipped to one knee.

That's when I got hosed again by the Sunset Strip villains. I got a short count. Six . . . seven at the most. A bit befuddled, I opened my mouth to protest the rip-off and I passed out luke-warm. The fight had been fixed. When I woke up the next morning, with a lousy hangover, I was chained up in the hold of the ship and my watch, cuff links, and sterling-silver ankle bracelet were gone.

Captain Engelhorn was ransacking my left armpit, something the skipper of the *Lusitania* would never do. Cheap boat, cheap help—and I could see that there wasn't much closet space either. I let out a small roar, which cracked Engelhorn's glasses and caught his attention. Being a person of no breeding, he also soiled his pants as he sprinted for the ladder to summon Carl Denham, prince of the low-low-low-budget quickies.

"I like your moves, Kid," he said, "and if you get your fangs capped you could go places. Who's your agent?"

"I'm self-insured."

He had a horrid laugh, and a million tricks. He also had plans, hemorrhoids, and debts that a couple of L.A. bookies were getting nasty about. It was his arms and legs or my ass . . . an easy choice for a producer.

"I'm going to make you a star, Kid," he promised slickly. "You'll be world famous, and you'll go out with broad-shouldered beauties in double-breasted jackets like Joan Crawford."

"How about Loretta Young?" I asked hopefully.

"My closest friend," he lied.

How could I know that a fine young actress like Loretta Young knew nothing of such vulgarians, or that his subsequent offer for me to play King Lear was an utter sham.

Tricked by this sly con-man, I offered no further resistance on the long voyage[k9] across the Pacific that ended on the docks of New York—only a few miles from the Empire State Building and that Broadway theatre.

[k9]The only good thing that happened on this journey was meeting the cabin boy who later became my best pal and literary collaborator. His brief comments in this book cover the trip more than adequately, but he always did run to excess.

Right from the start, I thought the costume was wrong. Who ever heard of King Lear in a black, fur jock with chains and metal bands holding him to a huge cross.

"Don't you get the symbolism? It's Lear as Christ!" Denham lied.

"Interesting," I mused.

Musing was one of the few things I could do all tangled up like that.

"Interesting? It'll be a sensation! And it'll pull in the S-M crowd," Denham predicted with a lewd chuckle.

"What about the critics?"

"*That's* the S-M crowd," he explained in tones dripping confidence.

I went back to studying my lines and had them letter pluperfect by the next night. You may not know this, but giant apes are very fast studies. We have top-notch memories, plus a lot of tolerance. Surely you've heard of the milk of apekindness. Well, it was dripping down my spats as I ran through Shakespeare's fine script with three girls in bunny outfits. I'd never heard of *Playboy*, so how could I guess that these stacked young females had been sublet by Denham to put me on?

They were one helluva improvement over Ann Darrow —at least in profile.

Okay, opening night.

"Have I gotten any wires?" I asked Denham with just a trace of opening night jitters.

"Golly, I left a bunch of them in my office. There was a great one from King Farouk of Egypt—a little porno but cute—and a neat one from the head of the orthopedics department at Bellevue hoping that you break a leg."

"Anything from my family?" I wondered hopefully.

"Someone named Rose sent a night letter from Philadelphia asking for six free tickets. A relative?"

"That's Mom!"

I sniffled shamelessly.

"You had a collect call from an Arthur Kong in London. I told him to shove it."

"That's Da-Da."

"Listen, Kid, the most important critics in the country are out there tonight. This is your big chance. Don't blow it. Give it plenty of fire, and roar a lot."

"You're sure that Lear would do that?"

"Absolutely. You're a king. Scream a lot!"

I believed him, since he was a pro and I'd never worked in anything but *Porgy* and some school productions of *The Mikado* financed by the Japanese Tourist Office. I was ready, and in my mind I could already see my name in lights. While I was getting myself in the mood and thinking "king" just as Stanislavsky recommended, Denham was ushering the reporters into the wings.

He was wearing a rented tux about two sizes too big, and they were wearing hats, cameras, and looks of lower-class stupidity. There wasn't an ounce of couth in the crowd, just brass and a tendency to speak too loudly in somebody's idea of Brooklyn accents. You can be sure that neither the New York or London *Times* was represented in that white trash. Most of them looked as if they couldn't find the bathroom . . . and had an urgent need to do so.

That has always been the greatest threat to a free press, but one must admit that it has helped the dry-cleaning industry. Well, Denham was smirking and curtseying shamelessly as he tried to curry favor[r-11] with those hacks by complimenting their shabby haberdashery and promising "a show that'll take the plaque off your teeth and the city editor off your backs."

With all due respect to the cultured members of today's Newspaper Guild, that simple-minded bunch at Denham's press conference had no idea what plaque was. In fact, they didn't know where they were. Somewhat disoriented by too much espresso, these were sports writers who thought they were at Madison Square Garden to cover the Joe Louis-Marcello Mastroianni heavyweight championship. Sports scribes have always suffered from a poor sense of direction and no sense of punctuation.

I wouldn't let my daughter marry one.

Which brings us to desperate Carl Denham's desperate ploy to inject some excitement into his trashy hype. "And here's the happy couple," he sang out with mock joy as he waved Ann Darrow and Brucie into the frame.

"Mon dieu, Marcello has lost a lot of weight," snapped the peckish wheat futures and physical-contact editor of the *Wall Street Journal*.

"Sacre du Printemps, schmuck," pecked the snappish lingerie and medical reporter for *Women's Wear* weakly, "that's Joe Louis in a witty blonde wig. He's so campy!"

"They're getting married and having kidney transplants," Denham boasted as he went into a quick buck-and-wing and a showy cerebral stroke. Then he cartwheeled onto the stage, unleashed several pretentious

[r-11]Or any other popular brand of wax.

105

remarks about the eighth wonder of the world and whipped back the curtain.

No warning. Lucky I wasn't scratching my ass or anything. What I was doing was looking around for Lear's daughters. Denham's invite to the lens lice to take pictures didn't bug me and neither did the flashbulbs. Friends, it never occurred to me that those lights might hurt Ann Darrow. Who cared.

What did occur to me was that I'd been had. All of a sudden it dawned on me that the whole Lear bit was a load of you-know-what and I'd been euchred like some dumb kid from the sticks.

I did what any self-respecting 132-foot[s] gorilla of mixed parentage would do.

I let out an indignant yell.

"Fraud! Sham! I've been screwed!" I called out righteously.

Unfortunately the cheap sound system at the theater completely distorted everything, so a lot of Cubans in the audience thought I was shouting "Remember the *Maine!*" and "Call the manager!" and they panicked.

"Where the hell's my daughter, Cordelia?" I inquired in a voice that shattered wine glasses in Baltimore.

"Taking a leak," Denham fenced.

He was lying, and I knew it.

He knew that I knew it, and I knew that he knew that I knew it. (You still with me? Hang on.)

I saw the Cubans, plus several Hungarians and some knowledgable-looking Choctaws bugging out, and I decided that they must know something I didn't. Maybe

[s]Okay, 131 feet 9½ inches.

the cops were going to bust the place—a grim prospect for a three-time loser like me.

First the credit cards.

Then the car keys.

Now my shot at King Lear.

Two of New York's top theater critics were dozing in the sixth row, center. The uproar awakened both gifted old farts at the same time, and it only took seconds for them to react.

"Could that baby play one terrific Lear!" judged the *New York Times* aesthete.

"So regal; a born king!" agreed the *Tribune* fop.

Encouraged by their sensitivity, I ripped out my shackles and tore loose so I could discuss the role with them.

Unfortunately, they were on fire due to someone's carelessness and they ran screaming from the theater. Sheep as all New York audiences are, everyone else set his/her clothes ablaze and docilely trotted out onto Broadway.

I went asking for the stage manager.

I had to take a leak myself (hardly surprising after thirty-two days and fourteen nights).

Nobody would talk to me—typical New York rudeness. I saw one overweight chap, whom I later learned was the fruit and nuts editor of *The New Yorker*, who seemed to know where he was going so I followed—hopefully. Quite unintentionally, I knocked out the rear wall of the building and found myself in the back alley.

I really should have paused, collected my wits, and taken stock.[M-3] Here I was in a strange and possibly dan-

---

[M-3]Xerox wouldn't be bad.

gerous place with hordes of disoriented sports writers, suicidal theater critics, neurotic audiences . . . and worse.

EEEEEK!

Roaches . . . armies of them, drilling in unison.

How was I to know that they were rehearsing for the Ed Sullivan TV show? There were no captions, just the haunting scent of Ann Darrow's exotic perfume in the night.

You think it was garbage? Maybe.

Whatever, I made up my mind to find Ann Darrow and ask her point blank about my car keys, which I'd certainly need to get home. All around me, people were running gaily into store windows (head on) and drivers were ramming expensive limos into walls and fire hydrants and the sweet sound of police sirens was everywhere. Since it was such a lovely night, I decided to walk.

In the movie, you then saw "me" wipe-out a crowded subway train running on elevated tracks twenty-five or thirty feet above the street. *That* wasn't me. *That* was RKO's thirteen-inch dummy. Completely innocent, I was blocks away sniffing for Ann Darrow. Once I thought I'd found her, but it was just the trash cans behind a taco parlor. Then I remembered that her Uncle Teddy owned the Shackup Towers Hotel, a mere two incredible strides over the pigeon-turded roofs.

With your gift of language, you could say that her odor drove me right up the wall. Actually, I had no choice. The freight elevator was ridiculously small, and I had no time [62] to horse around in the lobby. I smelled her perfume[63] and started casually up the side of the building.

[62] Also no change for the doorman.
[63] An odd Filipino brew named "Felonious Assault."

(Keep that in mind.) I was relaxed, jaunty, cool as a watermelon.

Perhaps you recall the next bit in the flick—the part where a giant gorilla reaches a massive paw into a room and pulls out a lady. Turns out to be the wrong one, so he drops her lots of floors to her violent demise. Again, *that* giant gorilla wasn't me. That was the thirteen-inch dummy, and the "lady" was an inch and a half Japanese doll —transistorized to the nipples. Damn clever those Nipponese, and awfully deft with their tiny nimble digits. Pretty good fiddlers too, even if not quite up to Zero's[64] standards.

Big Stan doesn't make such mistakes.

Great noses run in the Saperstein family, and in the Kong clan too. I wall-walked directly to the room where Ann Darrow and Bruce were . . . well, I never pry. They were in there alone, breathing hard and thinking slow and wondering whether the Supreme Being might strike them down for the crappy way they'd treated one of nature's gentlemen (*me*).

"Where the hell are the car keys?" I asked amiably as I rammed my enormous hairy paw into the room.

Don't ask me what she answered.

It's a shame. Both she and Cabot were high on something, and they shouted and hooted obscenities. It isn't easy to hoot one, not without special equipment and jungle boots. I figured she'd calm down if I got her alone and ripped off her jungle boots, so I flicked Brucie aside and scooped her out for a bit of fresh air.

She was screaming—and it wasn't the Radcliffe cheer. Let's face it. She was scared. The large question is

[64]Plays on roofs.

exactly what was it that so terrified a tough little veteran of show biz such as A. Darrow? It couldn't have been my fur because she had a mink coat and a chinchilla cape of her own, and it probably wasn't my obvious acting talent because her contract guaranteed her star billing.

A thoughtful writer and free-lance ape-ologist has faced this question squarely, roundly, and hexagonally in a superbly baroque essay[N11] titled "King Kong: A Meditation" that I could hardly understand. In fact, I don't remember it that well either, but he did raise at least two points worth considering. After that, he crapped out —as I recall.

His first point was: was Ann Darrow afraid of what might happen to her or what might not? Let me put it more tactfully. Was it fear or lust that caused her to make those crazy faces and holler so much? The author seems to suggest that she was hot to trot, eager to get down, and ready to go.

That's his idea not mine.

His second point was a whopper. He dares to ask the question that has been whispered in laundry hampers and ladies locker rooms for more than four decades. Why didn't they ever show my reproductive gear, and what were the dimensions thereof?

I have never discussed this in public before, but writers scribble about anything because they have wild imaginations, dirty minds, and insistent landlords. I don't intend to comment on what this chap wrote because I wouldn't dignify his speculations. I can report his estimate was six feet *inert*—twice that when aroused.

[N11] See pp. 131–137 in *The Girl in the Hairy Paw.*

Not bad, huh?

Six feet inert.

Twelve feet ert.

Moving right along, I climbed down the side of the hotel and looked around for a taxi. Not a cab in sight, but quite a few police cars four or five blocks away.

"Let's go up to my place, Big Boy," Ann Darrow whispered into my ear.

"Is that where the keys are?"

"Bet your huge furry rump," she giggled enticingly. "Turn right at Grand Central Station, and I'll guide you from there."

I didn't know the town, and I was eager to recover those keys and start home. I suppose that I should have suspected that I was being set up again, but I was only twenty and she was an older woman of the world. Foolishly trusting her, I followed her directions to the lofty structure that was then the tallest building in the world.

"I've got the penthouse, Baby," she cooed.

Up the side of the Empire State I climbed patiently. Up, up, up—and I wasn't even breathing hard. Everything was cool until we reached the eighty-eighth floor, when this little cutie began muttering something that I could barely hear in the high wind.

"Kongy honey, tell me. Where's Nicky?"

"Nicky who?" I answered as we reached the ninety-third.

"You know—good ol' Nicky and his Commie-rat friends?"

I thought it was altitude sickness making her talk crazy, so I decided to humor her.

"Give me those keys or I'll pulp you!"

"Nicky? Nicky? Nicky, Nicky, Nicky?" she persisted.

I put her down on the ledge up top, wishing she'd shut up. A moment later I saw her groping inside her dress.

"What's wrong, Pussycat?"

"I'm looking for my enema bag," she replied truthfully. (She didn't lie all the time.)

"You feeling sick?" I wondered solicitously.

The way she tells it, I solicited her wondrously—but that's a lot of crap.

"I've got to report to J. Edgar Hoover!" she shouted over the roaring wind.

(That woman was always so loud.)

I was unaware of the technical wizardry of American engineers and the marvelous patriotism of J. Edgar Hoover, the first to suspect Little Red Ridinghood, Red Grange, and the Scarlet Letter of Moscow sausage links and patties. Ignorant of the vast and secret ideological struggle between East and West, I thought Ann Darrow had lost her marbles as well as her enema bag and looked around for a phone to call the Menninger Clinic.

That was when I first spotted the airplanes.

Cheap old Curtis C-5 biplanes, as I recall.

World War I surplus junk we couldn't give away, so some sharpie unloaded those crates onto an RKO purchasing agent. Was it kickback time? We'll never know. Before I could price them out, the punch-drunk pilots swung-in to attack.

"Rat-tat-tat-tat!" crackled the machine guns.

I waved at them, and discovered that my paws were covered with grime from the outside of that dirty building.

"You got a john up here, Ann?" I asked and showed her my greasy paw.

She laughed—the little vixen.

What the hell was so funny? It was her penthouse, and she ought to know the layout.

"Rat-tat-tat-tat-tat!"

That was one more "tat" than before, and I felt a sting as bad as those big mosquitoes we had on Zumdum. There were two more "tats" the next time, and one tail-gunner gave an obscene hand-gesture. I returned the unidigit salute which later became popular with so many American students and politicians.

Lots more "rats" and "tats" until I remembered how Mom had taught me to cope with the mosquitoes. "Fart, Stan," she'd say, "it shows them you mean business." Worked like a charm. Blasted one of those obsolete biplanes out of the sky, and the others reeled back. But they weren't finished. I was bleeding a bit from eighty or ninety wounds, but holding my own . . . until they returned to attack again.

I could have handled them. I had some great moves I hadn't even used, but I didn't expect the old Samson bit. It was the skinny little broad who gave me the business. While my attention was focused on the planes, she crept up and tickled my right arch. I could never take that. Always broke me up. I began to laugh, and then I lost my balance—just for a second.

That did it.

Oooooooooooops!

There's one thing I can tell you about the Empire State Building.

That first step is a bitch.

Down, down, down—with those maniacs shooting at me all the way. There was also a cleaning woman who threw a bucket of dirty water into my face as I passed the fifty-sixth floor, and I noticed a man and a woman, at least fifteen years his junior, busy on a desk on the twenty-ninth. It could have been a medical research team.

Down, down, down . . . thump.

What a knock. It took the wind right out of me!

While I was lying there feeling absolutely rotten, Carl Denham came up with his usual crowd of bootlickers and studio cops. Not one of them offered me a hand or a glass of water. A gallon or two of Remy Martin, or Courvoisier, could have been a big help, but not from those Cossacks.

"Well, those planes really wracked up the old furball," one of the police smirked.

"Nah, nah, nah," answered Denham as he searched frantically for the cue-card. "Nah, it was beauty what killed the beast."

That's the kind of abuse I get all the time. Well, the movie gang packed up its gear and the crowd of thrill-seeking citizens departed. I was left lying there in the street. Gum, candy wrappers, dog turds, and cigarette butts everywhere. It was disgusting, and I was disgusted. When no ambulance showed up by one in the morning, I

114

scraped the crap off my fur and got up—quite irritated. With no help from anyone, I made my way to the out-patient clinic at Bellevue Hospital where a young interne named Darvon Ghandi examined me after a wait of only four hours. Ignoring the blood seeping from 124 bullet wounds, he made me stick out my tongue and read the eye-chart backwards. I was surprised to find that it was written in Urdu.

"You drink a lot?"

"I pee more."

"Eat a lot of spicy food?"

"Do I have to?" I asked.

He muttered something in Urdu and then mumbled in Hindi, and then chanted two ragas, one ashram, and a bangalore that I remembered from kindergarten in the swamp.

"Down with British Imperialism and curses to anyone who smokes Prince Albert," I agreed.

"There's nothing wrong with you that a hysterectomy or a long sea voyage won't cure, you lousy welfare fraud," he diagnosed as he relit his incense burner.

"You got anything cheaper, Sir?"

"Take five aspirins every ten minutes and get the hell out of here, malingerer."

He shoved two bottles of aspirin at me, kicked me in the ankle, and then kissed my toe with surprising affection. He was crying as I left . . . something from the Kama Sutra.

I swallowed the two bottles of aspirin—with the caps on—and wandered out into the street where I was promptly mugged. (Terrible neighborhood near Bellevue. They took my bridgework and the small toe off my left foot, which is why I still limp a bit.) Fed up with public hospitals, I trudged uptown and found a good general practitioner in the Bronx. He took out all the bullets, and told me not to worry if I couldn't pay his bill right way. He sold the slugs as souvenirs to collectors, deducted $75 for his services, and gave me the remaining $250 for walking-around money.

He also recommended a wonderfully well-dressed and aggressive lawyer; we sued the ass off the City of New York for malpractice, misdiagnosis, and sexual abuse. We won a judgment of a million four, of which my counsel grabbed half a mil. I don't begrudge him, but I do despise him a bit. It all happened quite a while ago, and there's been a lot of action in the outerim. The picture had its world premiere on March 2, 1933 in Los Angeles at Grauman's Chinese—where else? Two days later, it opened simultaneously at the Radio City Music Hall and the New Roxy's in Manhattan . . . and did capacity business at both. The film was a box office bonanza for RKO, did a lot for Fay Wray and as much as could be expected for Bruce Cabot who was still in trouble for letting down his country.

In a rare slip, RKO mistakenly picked a capable movie man to take over as chief of production—my pal Cooper. His pal immediately guessed that some other studio would try to rip-off the *Kong* success and came up with an imaginative idea. Why not rip off their own picture first? The result was a drag-ass schlepic titled *Son of Kong* which hung on a tiny twelve-foot ape they claimed was my offspring. That dreadful effort won Hollywood's coveted Silver Bedpan Award as the crappiest of the year. They took another game shot at gorilla thrillers in

1949 with *Mighty Joe Young,* a pleasant "B" film that cannot be compared with the majesty and tragedy of my screen debut.[862]

I stayed out of the movie business for a while, invested my money wisely in Arizona yoghurt groves that threw off a nice twenty-three percent each year. I married a couple of times and fathered eighty-three children—and not one of them a hippy. I took a whirl at politics and served for eight years in the California legislature, six in the U.S. Senate. Let's not rehash old wars and scandals. Over the years, I've grown mellow and used to a lot of things—even sadness when young girls refuse to play tennis with me. (In California, you're nobody if you're out of the tennis world.)

There's one thing that still bothers me: the discrimination against giant apes. There are fraternal orders honoring the moose, the elks, and the lions, but not one named for the simians. There are football teams celebrating tigers and bears, and there's even a baseball team named after the orioles.

That's just ridiculous.

Why not the gorilla?

I'll tell you why. Rotten press. We've always had unfair reporting, and a terrible image. We need to spend some money on public relations—like the whales. Do you think

---

[862]I gave the silver screen another chance in 1963 when I started in *King Kong vs. Godzilla,* a harmless Japanese romp that co-starred a young kid with horrendous breath. Fire shot from his mouth, and his posture was atrocious. I taught the kid plenty and gave him great tips such as look out for short agents. They always resent us big guys, and give the best deals to small folk such as Shirley MacLaine, Joel Grey, and Liza Minnelli.

it's an accident that everyone is suddenly all worked up about saving whales? Hell, no! It's $650,000 a year to a high powered p.r. firm that has great media connections. Everything's great about the whales, all positive.

"He's a whale of a guy," people say admiringly.

"He's a real ape," they say nastily.

Nobody cares about saving giant gorillas or making sure that we can get into West Point or the United Nations. We are beginning to see more gorillas in state legislatures and on the boards of trustees of some universities, and it's about time. We evade taxes just like everyone else, and we're entitled to equal everything. We're going to organize, a real lobbying outfit. My pal, that guy with the pegs in his neck who works up at the Frankenstein place, told me to get organized years ago.

"If you don't, the producers and garbage men will shove you all over the place and the zoo keepers will steal your bananas. Make noise," he groaned unintelligibly, "and remember it's the squeaky monster that gets the attention."

Damn right. That's what we're doing, and I'm confident that things will get better. At sixty-four—one year from Social Security—I take it easy, limiting myself to playing doubles and drinking triples. I've heard that a great Italian filmmaker is completing another big, big flick about your's truly, and I've benignly given him my blessing. No cash, though. I still don't quite trust that movie crowd, and I can't forget how RKO always filmed my bad side and Fay Wray's good one *and* never paid me a cent. I'm far from broke, you understand. The Good Lord has been good to me and the price of yoghurt is way up there and I cheat whenever I can—but I'm loyal to my

118

buddies. Not a Friday night goes by that I don't play poker with Dracula, that big-mouthed shark who made a bundle in *Jaws*, and a couple of the creatures from Outer Space who still moon about the casting cliques.

Then there's the kids.

I'm crazy about my children and my grand-children, especially proud of the furry one who's dean at a major medical school and never forgets his old grandad (or Jack Daniels either). Come Christmas, the whole family gathers at the ranch to pick the yoghurt and sing traditional Zumdum folk songs, plus some kazatzkas from Philadelphia and the Congo. Each year, we tell the same stories and sing the same songs and forge the same bills of lading.

Our heart-warming ceremony always starts the same way. The littlest sits on my lap, looks up appealingly and pleads.

"Ask the question, Gramps. Ask it, please?"

I smile, nod, puff on my cigar, and clear my throat.

It's the big moment, the thing that brings us together for another year—thank the Lord.

I clear my throat.

"Ann Darrow,"[q] I begin, and the tension is electromagnetic with reverse polarization.

"Did you ever notice she has shifty eyes?"

[q]Bless you, girl, wherever you are. I forgive you. Now . . . can I have my car keys?

119